"I won't tell anyone if y
out of my mouth before I c
swishes behind me as I step fi

Her eyes widen before they roam over my body with brazen appreciation. The act compels me to fidget with anxiety. The tip of her tongue touches her bottom lip, and her eyelashes flutter. I sit at her feet, and the fluttering stops. Her eyelashes lift to hit my face full blast with her stare again. She's practically panting with fear or something akin to it. We don't move but sit in the quiet while the party fades from the background to another plane.

"I'm reading." Her whisper is just as husky as mine. She delivers her words with a frown, but there's no fire behind them. "I don't like small talk, and I don't want to hear your war stories. I'm not going to be impressed."

"Then let's not talk." Three sentences in a row, and I'm home clear. I adjust my legs into a comfortable cross-legged position with my back to her. From this position, I can watch her reflection read in the window, hide from the party, and avoid disturbing her. I just hope she didn't detect my sigh of relief when she said she didn't want conversation. We sit in our quiet corner, but she doesn't return to her book. She's watching me as intently as I'm watching her.

Praise for Marilyn Barr

"The native mythology/elements were so well done, I found myself spellbound. Intricate descriptive narration that is not only historically accurate but believable makes this an incredible reading experience. Marilyn Barr is a gifted weaver of stories."

~ NN Light's Book Heaven
about Dance to a Wylder Beat.

"Marilyn Barr treats the reader to a fabulous trip back in time, capturing the simplicity, trials, and adventure of the early American mid-west....This is a beautiful literary tribute to the original peoples who called North America their home."

~ InD'tale Magazine about Dance to a Wylder
Beat, Crowned Heart Award Winner

Sound of a Wylder Silence

by

Marilyn Barr

The Wylder West Series

Sound of a Wylder Silence

Cover Art by *Tina Lynn Stout*

The Wild Rose Press, Inc.
PO Box 708
Adams Basin, NY 14410-0708
Visit us at www.thewildrosepress.com

Publishing History
First Edition, 2022
Trade Paperback ISBN 978-1-5092-4384-6
Digital ISBN 978-1-5092-4383-9

The Wylder West Series
Published in the United States of America

Dedication

To the Shamanic Practitioners who recovered my voice,
I am forever grateful to you.

Author's Note:

Sound of a Wylder Silence is a combination of significant research, my experience as a patient of a Shamanic healer, the experiences of my Native American colleagues in my meditation circle, and my imagination. I apologize in advance for any errors it may contain regarding Arapaho traditions. I only have the utmost respect for them and all the people in the Native American nations. I have done my best to give the Arapaho culture the respect it deserves, and any offense was not intentional.

Chapter 1

"I will believe you are a grown man when you don't have to remind me you are a grown man," my brother, Nartan, bellows. We have the same Arapaho almond-shaped eyes and raven's wing hair as our mother, but Nartan has the hard, cruel features of our father. He has needed those features to protect my softer, rounder ones in the past, but I'm done being his little project. We are only six years apart, but it might as well be a generation.

"Nartan, you were younger than me when you hunted buffalo. I should be able to decide whether or not I go to a Christmas party. We don't even celebrate Christmas. Why are you forcing this?"

"Because Olive wants it," he says with fire sparking in his eyes. "Olive wants you to see the others open the goods you made for them as presents for each other. She wants to introduce you to your clients and customers. Ikshu, I need you to take over your leather smith business before the babies are born. My heart cannot take her riding back and forth to town…even with you. I worry every second she is away."

There it is. Nartan's new bride, Olive Sagebrush, is the heart and soul of our little homestead and leather tanning enterprise. Now this argument makes sense. As much as Nartan has pushed for us to integrate ourselves into the town of Wylder and live as settlers, he wouldn't blow sparks at me for missing a party. The man has a hide thicker than a bull, but his soft spot for Olive makes him see red more often than not.

Olive won me over too. She has brokered deals with the gunsmith, the tobacco shop, the Wylder Store, and our skin traders in the Old States to sell my leather goods. She has turned my shameful hobby of "women's crafts" into a profitable business where I actively contribute to improving our homestead. I trusted her only moments after we met and haven't been disappointed once.

"A man would try, if not for himself but Olive." Nartan's voice softens. The sound is scarier than when he is yelling. He goes cold the way our father would when he punished the braves who would try to "toughen me up" for life in the Tomahawk Lodge.

Despite their efforts, I wasn't tough enough when the Shoshone brought the white man to destroy our circle during a buffalo hunt. I was the only able-bodied male there. I hid in a tree and brought shame to my family legacy…I wasn't old enough to wear tattoo rings, but it doesn't matter. Our people—old, women, and children—were slaughtered without hesitation. It was four years ago, in 1874, and miles away from Wylder, but the day took a piece of me in the form of my voice. Not talking has made me a burden to my brother when it doesn't have to be this way.

Now Olive wants me to peddle wares to the shop owners like a regular settler. I can't. I want to. I just can't be the voice of my company. How did I get myself into this mess? I look to my brother for sympathy and see the hardened determination of a newly married man with his eagle feathers for bravery dangling from his braids.

"I will go for Olive. I will show my face, but you cannot force my voice—"

2

"Ikshu—"

"I mean it, Nartan. You cannot force my voice because I can't force it. In this, I am as powerless as you."

****

"How was your train ride, Ava?" Dad's voice breaks the spell cast over me by the wilderness outside my childhood bedroom window. The relief I feel at being back in Wylder causes me to shake. I cannot cry because Dad will assume I want to go back to school. He would never guess that more than anything I want to miss today's Christmas party and find a tree to read beneath. I would need a blanket and little else to be at peace for a while. The promise of silencing the noises in my head is almost too much. The constant hum of conversations from the train car is still ringing in my ears.

"Uneventful," I reply with as even a tone as I can muster. School in New York is uneventful. My living arrangements in New York are uneventful. It was all uneventful until I received Dad's invitation to come home for Christmas. We have always been close, but I felt as if he had heard my prayers for a reason to leave New York. It is more than homesickness. How do I tell him I hate it there?

"That's the best type of journey. Excitement on a train usually includes robbers, breakdowns, or hot-tempered passengers. Ava, you know I would invite you home more often if I didn't worry about the journey itself."

"Oh Dad, it's not dangerous anymore," I say, fiddling with the lacy curtains at the window. "Everyone is civilized and restrained back east. No one puts up fists there. They backstab and manipulate the reputations of others instead. Their words are weapons, so pistols are no longer needed. Constant words blending into endless noise. I can hardly stand it."

I must have let too much of my bitterness show because Dad's bushy white eyebrows join the hair on his head. I can't look in his eyes and see the disappointment waiting there for me, so I focus on seeing my bedroom with new eyes. When I lived here, I couldn't wait to get out. The miles of pink lace on the bed, the canopy, and the curtains conspired to strangle me.

Even the hard surfaces aren't immune to a coating of pink lace. Lacy doilies are my sister's forte. I bet she's covering the English countryside in lace webbing, like a floral-scented spider. She's going to make a wonderful society wife and make Dad proud. While I resemble Abigail on the outside, I couldn't be more different on the inside.

"Well, I'm happy you are visiting. You bring life to this house like your mother used to."

Yep, that's me. I am the untamed daughter. Can I help it I was born to enjoy wide-open spaces instead of noisy parlors? While Abigail was setting up tea parties, I was climbing trees. She was always pouting when I received more adornments for my dresses because I created holes in them with my unfettered behavior.

She felt Mom and Dad were rewarding me for failing to be a lady, but I knew the truth. They were trying to put me on the path to an easier life than they had as settlers before the town of Wylder grew around them. Too bad the simple life they feel isn't good enough for me is what I have always wanted.

"Dad, I have been thinking about you living here alone." I test out my responsible tone of voice and attempt to channel my eldest brother, Finn. "Don't you think it would be prudent to have me here to help you around the house instead of in New York?"

"Princess, I don't need a babysitter. I'm not that old. I would never ask you to sacrifice your grand adventure to sit here and nursemaid me. I want you to find your way to nursing some younglings instead. The daydreams of grandchildren visiting Wylder in their city finery are enough to keep this old cowboy in the saddle." He holds his arms out, and I rush into his embrace. I hug my source of strength with all my might. I hope to inspire his thoughts of never wanting to let me go.

"Having children is far in the future, Dad." With the tears lodged in my throat, I sound more like a frog than his princess. He pulls me back to study my face, and I squirm.

"Not from where I'm standing, Princess. You grew up faster than the summer corn. Haven't you met anyone at school?" The concern in his eyes slices my heart to ribbons. I have met armies of suitors, but they are all hat no cattle. How do I tell Dad pompous gentleman bore me to tears?

"No one that can measure up to what you had with Mom. I'm serious when I say I want to stay in Wylder. I could help Finn with the mercantile and run this household for you. Cowboys ride through town all the time—"

"Some random cowboy isn't good enough for my little Ava Wylder," he says while holding my chin when I try to look away. "You are a jewel in the crown of the Wyoming Territory and were born to be a mistress of a fine manor, not a nursemaid for your dear ol' dad."

So much for the "helpful daughter" tactic. I can only

hope Finn falls for my plea to help take care of Dad. I'm going to have to step out of my comfort zone at this party and be social. I can trade one night of deafening noise and irritation for a lifetime of it in New York. If I can convince my brother I can make his life easier by staying in Wylder, I will create the alliance I need. My ticket from New York was one-way. By hook or by crook, I'm staying in Wylder.

****

Olive declared the decorations festive when we walked in, but I feel trapped. The floor-to-ceiling tree they brought inside serves only to make the space smaller. If they wanted a party decorated with pinecones, why are we inside? Instead, decorated pinecones laced with ribbons hang above us in garlands, bringing the ceiling lower. If settlers wore more practical sheepskin suits with fur boots instead of thin cloth, we could be outdoors where not only the people, but the air could circulate freely.

The combined smells of the food left sitting on tables for grazing oppress what little fresh air is captured in the schoolhouse. I labor to breathe. If someone talks to me, I may just faint like a swooning lady and never hear the end of it from Nartan. Even Olive would be laughing too hard at my peril to rescue me.

As soon as we enter the Wylder Christmas party, every settler freezes. Fear dances across the faces of every woman. Two oversized Arapaho Natives are usually cause for men to draw their women tighter and their hands to itch over their six-shooters. However, today is different because of a round-bellied loudmouth with a heart of gold. Olive pushes her way in front of us, igniting comfort and warmth throughout the room.

"Sorry, we are late. I don't move as fast as I did five months ago," Olive says loud enough to drown out the crowd. She rubs her enormous belly for emphasis. The scorn falls from the settler's faces at the innocent statement of the deceptively tiny woman. My sister-in-law is the most lethal of our family, which is probably why my brother's eyes are twinkling with amusement. Olive is Ephraim or a she-bear shifter. When she and Nartan told me her secret, I thought they were pulling my leg, until she shifted and nearly roared my hair off.

"Olive, I have someone I'd like you to meet." Gotti, the butcher and our closest friend, waves us from the doorway to the punch table. Here we go. My first trial already. Gotti has traded cow brains for young lambs with Nartan since we moved here four years ago. He set up the arrangement between Nartan and the stockyard to give us the skins of any passing cows for our leather tanning business. We tan the hides and send them to the Old States via train. When they wire us payment, Nartan gives a share to the stockyard.

"I'm on my way, sir. It may not look like it at my pace, but I'm skedaddling," Olive calls while making a show of waddling for the giggling crowd. My brother clutches her hips as if to carry her across the room until she swats him away. The moony eyes he's giving her turns my stomach more than the smelly buffet. I waver between puzzlement, nausea, and green-eyed jealousy at my brother's behavior. If I can retrieve my voice, perhaps Nartan would help me telegraph for a catalog bride too. I would love to have an Olive for my own and not just because she would do all the talking.

"This is Anastasia West, my intended, and our friends George McIntyre and Allie Murphy," Gotti says

7

to bring me back to the present. Without missing a beat, Olive shakes their hands, and Nartan follows suit. Gotti and Olive are probably the most outgoing, friendly people on the planet. She jabs me in the ribs hard enough to knock the air from my lungs when I hesitate to join in.

"Mighty fine to make your acquaintance. This is my husband, Nartan, and his brother, Ikshu." The love shining in her eyes as she loops her arm around my brother is astounding. How did he get someone to look at him like that with his temper? Jealousy surges to the forefront when I realize I am surrounded by newlywed or about to be wed happy couples. The only thing worse is if someone—

"Ikshu the craftsman. I just love the holster I got from Cyrus. In fact, I bet you a mutton chop he corners you to ask for larger shipments at the party. He is around here somewhere," Gotti cranes his neck to try to spot Cyrus among the partygoers. *Please do not bring more people into our tiny part of the room.*

"Thank you for the compliment, Gotti," Olive says while waving her eyebrows in my direction. That's my cue. I'm genuinely pleased he likes my work, so I need to tell him. I need my mouth to function. Seconds tick by as I fight with my vocal cords. Is everyone staring or just my family? *Sigh.* Olive called attention to me and now everyone is watching my fish impersonation. Open. Close. No sound emerges. My mind spins and then the floor does as well. I send a prayer to my ancestors to hold my belly contents within my person. By some miracle, I smile and nod to the group without decorating the floor.

"How long have you been settled in Wylder?" George thankfully asks the question in Olive's direction instead of mine.

"We settled about an hour's ride west of here almost five years ago. Olive joined our family last summer," Nartan's authoritative voice rumbles over our heads. It brings me back to our tribal circle where Nartan would speak for me as much as possible. He has always been taller than me with the same wide shoulders and imposing build. From the outside, I seem the perfect brave from good stock. Too bad I could never fill the shoes while being true to myself.

As the couples chat in a circle, I inch backward to fade into the decorations. The group closes ranks and hardly notices my absence. Each lady steals adoring glances at their man between additions to the conversation. They laugh, smile, and gesture with increasing giddiness. Over their heads, each man gazes down with pride. I wish to join them, but I'm missing more than manners.

With confidence they have forgotten me, my steps grow. A hole has formed over my heart. If we hadn't been cast out of our tribal circle, I would be married already. I would have earned feathers on the battlefield or at least my tattoo rings hunting buffalo. With the interference of the US Government, buffalo hunting parties are illegal.

Tribes are still warring, but Nartan promised Sorrel Horse we would join Wylder as settlers instead of staying on the reservation. At the time I was happy to get away from the braves who taunted me for being soft and making the jewelry they wear in the ceremonies. Now I am at a loss without the rites of passage to transition from boy to man. Without feathers, tattoo rings, or buffalo pelts, how will I gain independence from my brother?

"*Oomph*, pardon me." The gruff voice comes from

a scarred settler slightly taller than me. This must be another close friend of Olive's, Cyrus the gunsmith. It would be an outstanding first step if I could make his acquaintance on my own since he appreciates my work. I open my mouth and feel the crushing weight of embarrassment when nothing emerges.

"Are you Ikshu Sagebrush?" The kind man puts me out of my misery. I am relieved until internal questions about how much Olive has told him threatens to double me over with intestinal cramping. She wouldn't tell my secrets on purpose, but she is a blabbermouth.

I nod to Cyrus and offer my hand. He shakes it heartily while rocking his glass of punch in his other hand. I can't look away from the liquid swirling in his cup. Will it spill, or will the cup height be enough to contain his drink? When it settles, I realize Cyrus is still talking to me. What have I missed? Oh please, don't ask me anything.

"Those holsters flew off the shelves, even the ones for ladies. I bet half the presents over there are your creations. You must be excited for everyone to open them."

I smile warmly and nod at his praise. I am excited about the presents but not for myself. Nartan sent for a special gold wedding ring for Olive from the Old States. While I'm jealous I don't have someone to give a golden ring, the present will mean the world to the brother who dedicated himself to raising me when our parents left this world.

"Well, as soon as you make another bundle, I want you to refill my window. I thought this was a nice thing to do for your family, but it is turning into a profitable enterprise for both of us. Here's to a long partnership,"

Cyrus says, raising his glass overhead. The liquid swirls vigorously and, this time, sloshes over the side and onto our shoulders. The punch rolls off my tanned leather but soaks into his shirt, leaving a pink circle.

"I'm so sorry. Did I get you?"

"It rolls off sheepskin as it is naturally waterproof." My voice startles me more than Cyrus as he rubs his shoulder vigorously with a napkin. "Here, just unfurl the ribbing on your vest and no one will see it." I adjust both shoulders and obscure the stain. I glow with pride. I spoke to someone!

"Thanks, I mean it. Get to work and see you soon in the smithy."

"I will," I whisper, but proud that the words left my lips. As he disappears in the direction of my family, I can only hope they ask after me. It will knock them flat if Cyrus says he already spoke to me. Doesn't that have a ring to it? I already spoke to Cyrus…on my own…without my pushy sister-in-law or domineering brother.

With my duty completed, I gaze over the presents. I should be sizing them up for the number containing Sagebrush leather goods, but old habits die hard. I spy a hiding place just my size. Between the red wool curtains, the high back cushioned chair, and the taller presents, I bet I could spend the rest of the evening alone. Using stealth usually reserved for the forest, I creep behind the tree and squat within the curtains to watch the first flakes swirl in the night.

****

It is so loud here. Why is everyone talking at once? They can't possibly hear each other over the din of the crowd. I thought I was handling everything wonderfully when we arrived early to put out the buckets of peppermint candy from the Wylder Store. Then the guests arrived…and kept arriving…and arriving.

By the time the children's choir sang at seven, the schoolhouse was packed. Their rendition of "Silent Night" warmed my heart, mostly because the crowd was quiet to listen to it. It gave my poor senses a rest. Then it happened. Someone armed the little vipers with bells. I'm still freezing from slipping outside until Violet, their teacher, thankfully confiscated the torturous instruments.

Dad is proud as punch telling stories to those little kids by the stove, but he tells it at maximum volume to be heard by the youngsters. I bet their parents are grateful for a few minutes of kid-free fun or maybe the rest of the night with the way Dad carries on. While I love his stories, I have heard them over a million times.

This particular one is about the outlaw he found hiding in our barn who held him at gunpoint until Mom came in yelling about being late for breakfast. She hit the man over the head with a frying pan and knocked him out. They tied him up and then didn't know what to do. There was no sheriff in those days.

Mom came up with the idea to put him in a boxcar on the next train. With a bucket of fresh water and a bundle of Mom's homemade hot rocks, they sent him on his way to the coast. That was Mom though, a wild woman who would take on a gun shark with a frying pan but then give him a hearty breakfast when sending him away.

Dad got to the part where he was held at gunpoint when I made my move…I spied the high back chair facing the window as my perfect hiding spot the moment we arrived. Becoming invisible is the most useful skill I acquired at school. I can hide like a rabbit evading a mountain bear. In New York, parties like these are for hunting spouses. The men in New York are educated, well-spoken, and handsome, but that is all they are.

If they were held at gunpoint like Dad, they would talk the outlaw to death or perhaps just wet themselves. Certainly, none of them would be grateful to be rescued by their wife and then conspire to send the scoundrel away on a random train like partners in crime. The only way to avoid a shouting match with the blowhards was to find a quiet hiding spot and put my nose in a book. My dream man would not only have the adventures from my books but allow me to participate, like the poem I just finished reading, "The Owl and the Pussy Cat."

Despite my new commitment to integrating into Wylder and establishing myself at Dad's side, I couldn't leave my new book *Around the World in Eighty Days* at home. I read *Journey to the Center of the Earth* and *Twenty Thousand Leagues under the Sea* monthly at school. Those adventures between the pages kept the tears away. The day my train was due to leave for home, Jules Verne's newest book arrived in the school's library.

I couldn't believe my luck when I stumbled over it before it could be tagged and inventoried. Slipping it from the stack of mail and into the folds of my traveling dress had been almost too easy. It was as if I was destined to steal it. Now that I have it safe in Wylder, I can't resist a little peek while Dad is otherwise occupied.

By the end of chapter one, I am transported to the rousing card game in the book. I almost escaped when cackling laughter brought me back abruptly. *Sigh*, perhaps I will never have the privacy needed to enjoy myself. The mixture of conversations batter inside my head with little hammers. Why is it I can never avoid the constant talking of others? Is there really so much to say? I could enjoy my book, the party, and the first few flakes of snow outside if everyone would just stay quiet.

This book has brought forth memories of playing cards with the maids at school. My roommate, Cecilia, introduced me to playing cards, smoking cigars, and many other pastimes that would make Dad blush and my brothers fly through the roof. If only I could leave for a trip around the world, like the male characters in my books. I'm brought out of my trance by the rustling of wrapping paper and the clapping of ornaments on the tree. *Sigh*, one of the kids escaped and now has found my hiding spot. *Great.*

"Clear out, or I will tell Santa you tried to run away and join a circus," I scold the shape hiding in the curtains.

****

I didn't mean to intrude upon the woman perched in the chair, but once I found her I couldn't move. She looks like the angel at the top of the Christmas tree come to life. The familiar paralysis in my mouth spread through the rest of my body as I tried to absorb everything about the delicate woman hiding in the high back chair.

She curls into a ball to make herself as small as possible, her feet tucked beneath the lacy hem of her storm-cloud gray dress. Eyes of a matching hue dart over the pages of her book while a smile tugs on the right corner of her lips.

Whatever is written on those pages builds excitement within her bosom, if the fluttering of the white lace at her neckline is any measure. With each exhale, the golden tendrils which have escaped the knot at the back of her head wave from under her chin. I'm held in place by her stare as she growls her ridiculous warning. Living with Olive the she-bear, this angel is as frightening as a prairie flower.

"I won't tell anyone if you won't." The words fly out of my mouth before I can stop them. I'm not proud of the husky whisper I use to deliver them, but they came out. The curtain swishes behind me as I step from behind it. The tree obscures my view of Olive and Nartan. Hopefully, it blocks their view of me as well. My gut instinct says what I'm about to do is beyond stupid.

Her eyes widen before they roam over my body with brazen appreciation. The act compels me to fidget with anxiety. The tip of her tongue touches her bottom lip and her eyelashes flutter. I sit at her feet, and the fluttering stops. Her eyelashes lift to roam my face with her gaze again. She's practically panting with fear or something akin to it. We don't move but sit in the quiet while the party fades from the background to another place.

"I'm reading." Her whisper is just as husky as mine. She delivers her words with a frown, but there's no fire behind them. "I don't like small talk, and I don't want to hear your war stories. I'm not going to be impressed."

"Then let's not talk." Three sentences in a row, and I'm home clear. I adjust my legs into a comfortable cross-legged position with my back to her. From this position, I can watch her reflection read in the window, hide from the party, and avoid disturbing her. I just hope she didn't detect my sigh of relief when she said she didn't want conversation.

We sit in our quiet corner, but she doesn't return to her book. She's watching me as intently as I'm watching her. Minutes pass. Her mouth opens and closes as if she has reconsidered her offer of silence, but she doesn't disturb me. The music fades to nothing. The world seems to stop while waiting for one of us to open up.

When the other partygoers approach the tree to pass out presents, I lift them from my hiding spot to keep her from being discovered. She shrinks into the chair with a conspiratorial smirk that shouldn't make my insides glow the way they do. No one asks after a lost family member. There are no presents for her. A rock sits over my heart. I have so many pretty things in my teepee, but I didn't think to bring any of them. It is not like anything I make could measure up to the finery she is currently wearing.

"Olive, this vest is amazing," a man's voice projects from the other side of the tree.

"Ikshu made it. He makes all our leather goods by hand and does the beading too. He's an artist. Ikshu, where are you?"

I lean around the tree to wave at Olive and the man holding the vest against his chest. My measurements were a bang-up job, and it will fit him like a glove. I smile with happiness at my handiwork. The angel in the chair watches my interactions as if I'm the most interesting person at the party. I don't wish to give away her hiding place, but my eyes seek her expressions like the deer to a watering hole. Try as I might, I must always return to her face.

I get complimented by several settlers for making the gifts they give to one another. This is a far cry from the ridicule I have received most of my life. While my talents have never been denied, no one has ever encouraged me to pursue them. In my culture, they are too feminine. To each amazed settler, I wave, shake hands, or nod with ease. I'm not talking, but I'm surrounded by people fawning over me without passing out. I've made progress, right?

Olive squeals loud enough to bring the house down when Nartan gives her the ring. I peek around the tree a second time to spy on my brother and his wife. They are surrounded by laughter when he slips the ring on her finger. It fits, and I pat myself on the back for not only calculating the size correctly for him but also selecting a design she wouldn't refuse.

When they married last summer, she insisted on the traditional tattooed ring. Now Nartan has his way as usual with this ring as a "Christmas present" when neither of them has ever celebrated Christmas.

In my spying, I forget my proximity to the high back chair and the silent lady within it. I'm nearly draped over her. I jump back as if the chair is on fire, but it is just my cheeks flaming with embarrassment. "Sorry," I mouth in her direction.

"I'm not, Ikshu. I'm Ava," she whispers the words before slipping her stocking feet into fancy settler shoes. The wet, cold ground will seep through those flimsy things. She needs to be wearing boots to keep her feet dry. Warm boots to lovingly cocoon her feet, not low-cut leather with gaping holes for buttons. I'm so busy judging her shoes, I miss her cue to take her hand.

I'm shocked to my toes when her slender fingers, encased in soft cotton gloves, wrap themselves around my calloused hand and use my strength to lift her from the chair. I'm as animated as a tree stump with panic. Is she so close to squeeze by the tree or drive me crazy with the floral scent of her hair? She lifts my arm and slides

17

underneath it. The action rubs her torso along mine as she steps at an angle. For a split second, my leg is between hers, and the intimacy brands me with her imprint. I gasp in shock to get a nose full of violet and vanilla from her hair.

"Merry Christmas, Ikshu." She whispers the endearment below my ear before collecting an old man from beside the fireplace and walking outside with her head held high.

Once outside, she turns to the window as if she knows I am watching. I lift my hand to the frigid glass. "Merry Christmas, Ava," I whisper to the window.

Chapter 2

Step one—light the calumet, even if it is Nartan's stolen pipe. Step two—dance. What do I do with the pipe while I dance? If I get lost in the spirit, I will burn myself with it. I know it. I wander around our barn looking for clues to his ritual. I find three horses housed in four stalls, the old can, and a ton of manure. Nartan must light the pipe and then set it in the can to smoke as an offering while he dances.

I only wish I would have learned as many steps as my brother. I was still newly accepted into the Star Lodge when we left the tribe. Nartan had finished his Star apprenticeship with a Shaman, had several vision quests, and took several trips to Sun Dance. He also had the opportunity to learn from the braves of the Tomahawk Lodge, even though his path pointed to being a medicine man rather than a hunter.

"Those who are enlightened may enter, and those who are unenlightened must go, for I am creating a sacred space." I have heard Nartan call to his guides while hidden beside our barn at least a thousand times. Each greeting is the same with the precision only a spiritual ritual would require. However, I have never seen what happens next. I haven't dared tempt the wrath of my brother to peek between the crooked slats on the barn.

"Oh Nartan, why does this work for you and not

me?" I yell my question to the heavens with only a small hope of his appearance. Perhaps my concentration is the problem. I burnt my candle to its base and then used the sunrise to sew all night long. The result of my labor is the finest pair of rabbit fur boots this side of the Mississippi. Now the hitch in my wagon is not having the courage to give them to their new owner. My recent obsession with a pair of gray eyes has given me the courage to steal his calumet.

"You need to make your own pipe to call your teacher first. Your sacred space is hardly large enough to hold one of our sheep, but until you have a teacher who can call in your spirit guides, you will be alone in the space."

Well, speak of the devil. "Whatever you say, you can manifest" is an old Arapaho saying I need to embrace. Olive likes to tease Nartan by talking about having many children as often as she can. The night they were married, she manifested a dozen newborns…lambs, that is. I was alone to start the birthing process with our ewes and young. When Olive took over in the middle of the fiasco, I couldn't help but marvel at her natural maternal instincts. I just manifested my brother and, probably, his temper by thinking about his growing family in a sacred space.

"How do I call in my teacher?"

"You don't call them in. You travel to their plane and seek guidance. One of the spirits will claim you." Nartan leans casually on the towering hay. We bartered with a neighboring ranch for the two-story stack with a bucket of my handmade brushes.

I can't ask merchants around town to sell my art and I'm supposed to ask around the spirit realm for a teacher?

I puff out my cheeks in exasperation. There has to be another way. "Will you help me astral travel?"

"No."

"Come on, Nartan, I went to the stupid party and talked to people at your request. Why won't you help me?"

"Number one, I can't help you. It is a vision quest you take on your own when you are ready. The whiny tone in your voice tells me you aren't ready. Harvesting fruit before it's ripe will only leave you with a bitter taste in your mouth, Ikshu. Why rush it?"

"You said that malarky is number one. What's reason two?"

"Olive wants you to accompany her to town. She needs to visit the dress shop, and when I asked to take her she said no. She suggested you drop more holsters to the gunsmith right around the corner. I couldn't figure out if she was embarrassed by her dress shop needs or if she really wanted your company over mine."

I throw my head back and laugh at my scary brother. For all his adornments for bravery, spiritual visions, and leadership from his earlier days, he is scared to death Olive will find him unworthy and leave. Perhaps it would be best for both if they fill the house with children, just so my brother is secure in their relationship.

"Nartan, Olive only has eyes for you. You saw her at the Christmas party. Merchants, cowboys, and gentlemen asked her to dance. She hung on you all night, claiming her feet were too swollen. When has Olive ever passed up on the chance to dance?"

"True. I would fall apart if I lost her again, Ikshu." The truth in his eyes is heartbreaking. The last time Olive ventured into town alone, she was assaulted by a gun shark. Nartan thought he lost her, but the gun shark ended up getting the business end of her black bear. My brother snapped, and only the love of his wife put him back together.

"Then I better gather my wares for a trip to town. I'm sure it's women's stuff and has nothing to do with us." I am walking away from Nartan before the words leave my lips. If he's going to ignore my theft of his pipe, all the better. I'm not calling his attention to it.

Back at my teepee, my gaze is drawn to the light gray fur-lined boots I have painstakingly created overnight. Rabbit fur not only lines the tops but reaches the toes and hugs the inner workings of the heels. No detail is left to chance. I even sewed tiny pink bone beads into rosettes on the ankles. Wood frames widen the base slightly, but the tops are wrapped in rabbit skins so they cannot be seen.

These will not only keep Ava warmer than her settler boots, but she will be less likely to slip on the ice. I made them taller than I would normally dare so the insulation will continue beneath the hem of her skirt and there is no chance of a draft. Hopefully, Ava is a woman daring enough to wear such tall boots.

My confidence falters when I load the travois hitched to the back of my horse, FoolsGold. What if Ava hates the boots? What if she counts on societal fashion to feel confident and I destroy it by offering Arapaho style boots? From the way her eyes appraised me, I doubt she has a prejudice toward me, but do her feelings extend to my art?

FoolsGold senses my mood and bucks hard enough to bang the travois poles on the ground. The long poles extend from around his neck and cross over his back to about a man's length behind him. Leather is stretched between the two poles to carry the load while lofted knee-high off the ground. Usually, Olive's horse, Strawberry, carries the load, but with Olive pregnant we aren't taking chances on Strawberry staying calm. Horse and rider have had a tenuous relationship at best. I'm waiting for the edict handed down from Nartan saying Olive is no longer allowed to ride. Afterward, there will be fireworks when Olive sets him straight.

"You ready, Ikshu?" Olive waddles down the steps of her cabin on the hill at the western edge of our property. Also on the hill are our chicken coop and garden before the land becomes a forest of spruce trees we debark for smoking. An ankle-deep tributary of the Medicine River cuts our land in half next, with smokehouses, tanning frames, and soaking vats along its edges. On the far side, and downwind of the urine vats, is our barn and original teepee. Since Nartan moved in with Olive, I have stayed in the teepee, but it may be time for my arrangement to change.

"I can bring the horses to get you. You don't need to cross our entire homestead to ride back to the road."

"I got tired of waiting. Plus, walking is good for babies. It makes them stop kicking."

"Babies and not the baby?"

Olive's eyes fill with a mischievous twinkle. "Oh yes, I am carrying babies. Any baby kicking this much will be too ornery for me to handle. I keep saying babies to make my intentions clear."

After a chuckle, I boost her into the saddle on Strawberry. She winces, but I know better than to inquire into her well-being. I've heard her rail at my brother from outside their cabin and across the tanning yard to my teepee. She doesn't take kindly to being limited by her condition and is vocal against the delicate treatment my brother is trying to enforce upon her person.

"Shake a leg, Ikshu. There's a fortune to be made."

"Nartan mentioned the dressmakers as well," I say while swinging into my saddle and avoiding the travois.

"Never you mind. I will be visiting Mrs. Lowery for some unmentionables and I do not wish to discuss them with you. This will be the fourth time in as many months I will be buying such wares from her establishment on account of your brother's eager nature. I can't believe I have to go in there shamefaced again. You sass me about this, and I will drag you in there too. Spread my misery."

"Yes, ma'am," I say to avoid the dressmaker's shop. If I can usher Olive inside the establishment, I can give the boots to Ava without Olive knowing. As much as I would like Olive's advice on whether Ava would like the boots, I am not ready to share our private moment at the Christmas party with my sister-in-law.

"I mean it, Ikshu," Olive continues as if I hadn't answered. "Do you believe the last visit she asked me if I should be having *that caliber of relations* in my condition? I felt no taller than a bug and about as filthy as one as well."

I hold my tongue because nothing I can say would further my cause. Arapaho women do not usually wear such things, but Olive probably knows already. She wears them to please my brother. I can only hope no one gets it into their head for me to make them. I may be versed in sewing and beading, but I'll be pickled before I sew entertainment for my brother.

Chapter 3

They must have come from him. There is no note or tag, so it could be wistful thinking on my part. Ikshu, the leatherworker, must have made these boots with his bare hands. Abandoned on our stoop this morning, I know they are for me. The only other person living here is my dad, and he wouldn't wear something so delicate, even if they fit him. The caring wrapped within the gray fur is more than my logical conclusion though.

Just the thought of placing my bare feet where his hands have been makes my heart flutter. I moan quietly as I slip my foot into the furry interior. How decadent to have lavish fur where only I know it is there. He has embraced me with warmth and protection from afar. The private gift of giving me comfort without showing it to others is almost too much. The boots are tall enough to massage my calves with each step as if he is rubbing my legs beneath my skirts. How deliciously indecent!

I run my hands over the fur on the outside while thinking of the brazen act of putting my gloved hand in his uninvited at the party. He froze and let me take the lead. I was limited only by what I thought was proper, and wasn't that heady? I lay on my back porch and lift my booted feet to the sky to gaze upon them. Laundresses bustling in and out of the stacks of clothes behind our house will not spoil my moment. Wylder isn't nearly as crowded as New York, but I yearn for wide-open spaces, nature, and most of all, silence.

Ikshu is a master of quiet. At the party, I hardly heard him breathe when I said I didn't want to talk. I kept waiting for him to break the silence with some stupid boastful story. He never did, and it left me wanting—*the devil.* Could he be sitting in a teepee somewhere sewing boots for all the ladies in town, or is this act of kindness special? Perhaps he is ranching at Circle W as a laborer and makes the leather goods on the side. If I rode out to the common green, will I find him astride a stallion— dare I say riding bareback?

A vision of Ikshu on a stallion rearing back floats through my mind. His hair isn't braided in my fantasy but fanned into wings of silk trailing behind him. He isn't wearing the decorative smock he wore to the party either. *No.* His broad shoulders, wide chest, and strong arms would be on display as he reins in the dangerous animal. *Sigh.* He would ride over to me and lift me on the horse with one arm. I would throw my arms around his neck. Our mouths would meet in a tangle of frenzied passion.

Fueled by my imagination, I charge toward our rented stalls in the town's livery. Lady is where I left her but excited to see me. Since Abigail and I have been at school, our horse, Lady, has been relegated to pulling our wagon. The excitement builds in her as I brush her and prepare her for the saddle. She is as thrilled to be on an afternoon ride as I am. She scuffles and dances as I coo to her to settle.

"Whoa, I'm rusty," I say to the skittish mare as I mount. I wobble in my saddle, nearly grassing myself to the backside and the front. In New York, a proper lady uses horses to pull her carriage, not to sit astride. Since I didn't wish for the lavish library at my fingertips to go to waste, I rode when invited for social purposes, and then it was a quiet promenade with some suitor who was trying to impress the "girl from out west."

I longed for time with Lady to tear off along the prairie in search of adventure. I pitch and lurch in my saddle with every step along Old Cheyenne Road until I am hidden behind the Calvary Office.

"You know what, Lady? No one is watching us here, and no one will be the wiser. Can you keep a secret?" She grunts with impatience and swings her body. Another almost ejection firms my resolve. I tuck my skirts between my legs and swing astride.

"Let's go." The words hang on my lips as Lady tears off across the open prairie to the village green. The crunch of dormant plants adds staccato notes to the pounding of her hooves. Shades of brown are dotted with green tufts of sagebrush, which infuse the prairie with their spice.

I pull the clean air greedily into my lungs and match Lady's breaths. For once, I am free, and it brings tears to my eyes. They dart down my cheeks. The cold threatens to freeze them solid before they whip behind us. I don't dare let go of the reins to claw them away and risk injury at this high speed.

Luckily, she loses steam before we reach the village common green, which is looking quite common but not very green. A sea of cattle ambles along the pasture adorned with a rider here and there to keep the beasts in line. I recognize none of them, but why would I? I have changed in the months since I have been in New York. Why shouldn't Wylder grow up too?

Fletcher's warnings about being on the green alone echo in my ears as I nod at each ranch hand who tips his hat to me. These aren't familiar faces but faces of all colors and shapes, hardened with the lines of rough living and weary travel. I am outnumbered. I am alone. I shiver on my mount and question the wisdom of such a bold move.

"Fletcher is just trying to scare me into obedience." I punctuate the statement with an inelegant snort. I guide Lady to the tree line at the edge of the green and dismount. I tie her loosely to an old cottonwood tree with a limb sturdy enough to hold my weight at waist height.

"I refuse to be thwarted by silly fears. I have a book, a blanket, and a means of escape. We are going to enjoy ourselves. Right, Lady?"

Lady grunts between tired pants. I hug her neck before climbing into the tree. Crossing my ankles around my perch for stability, my attention is drawn to my beautiful new boots. My blanket and dress are pine green, so I blend in with the surroundings.

Maybe I didn't lead myself to certain peril after all. Any other season and I would be hidden completely. Who knows? Maybe Ikshu will save me from miscreants like a white knight from my books.

Minutes tick by, but I can't focus on the words on the page. Even the camel rides of Phineas Fogg cannot hold my attention. There is a niggling feeling in the back of my mind. I am missing something. I gaze along the rolling brown backs of the Texas Longhorns to the black lumps of Angus. None of their handlers look appetizing in the least. Beyond the furthest herd is a small flock of sheep, filled with dancing juveniles. I'm not sure which is funnier—the clumsy gait of the lambs or the tactical movements of their handler. The man is as broad as he is tall upon his Missouri Fox Trotter. Even Lady perks up at the sight of him in recognition of a male horse of the same breed.

"Oh yes, Lady. They make for fine entertainment, don't they? If only I had some glasses or the will to move them closer, for the rider is without shirtsleeves." I rub my hands together and blow into them. Why didn't I bring gloves?

We watch in fascination as rider and horse corral the unruly flock. As frantic as the juvenile sheep move and bounce, the driving pair is steady and methodical. Their coordinated rhythm assures no energy is wasted until the group is maneuvered to the edge closest to my tree.

I rub my hands together for the thousandth time to thaw them with enough vigor to jostle the book from my lap. It falls to the ground with a thud that joins the chorus of bleats and moos on the prairie.

I'll get the book when I leave, I guess. It is getting too cold for me to stay much longer without gloves. *Sigh.* I lean against the tree, blow into my hands, lift my gaze back to the sheepherder…

…who is watching me intently.

Rounding his herd, I get an intimate view of my eye candy. Ikshu's vest is indeed sleeveless, and his arms are the circumference of my tree-branch perch. The rolling muscles draw my eye to the sheepskin vest which is covered with colorful symbols. *Sheepskin*. Of course, he wouldn't have a cattle flock if he has a business in leather goods. He could barter for hides from the surrounding ranches and stockyard, but sheepskin would be a special commodity he would need to supply for himself.

He tips his hat and sends me a wink that awakens my spirit. My face stretches while I send him a wave with my ungloved hand. Time slows as he removes a cuff from his forearm, just below his elbow, and secures the clasps into a circular shape. Using his powerful legs—that I only noticed because I was admiring the quality of his sheepskin leggings…like a lady—he guides his horse to the opposite end of the branch where I sit.

I'm captivated as he bends the thin tree tip to eye level and threads the arm wheel over it. When he releases the twig, it snaps upward and the cuff shoots along the branch. The red, blue, and orange beads blend into streaks of fire as it spins toward me.

It stops nestled between my boots with a delicate clink. As if compelled by a divine force, my fingers lovingly caress the beadwork. There is an orange phoenix with dark red wings in the mosaic. It is the most beautiful gift I have ever received.

I remove the cuff from the branch and check his expression for acceptance. This was for me, right? His face is rounder than I remember from the party. Kinder with an easy smile framed with lines of maturity. His eyes are mysterious pools of warm brown, so dark they are nearly black.

Are you a gentleman or a scoundrel, my wild admirer? He tips his hat politely. Before I can stop myself, I blow him a kiss. He startles, and his horse side-steps. I am captivated as he calms his stead, turns, and guides his flock to the south.

"Please turn to wave. Come on. Please turn back," I whisper as the sheep leave the green. I get my wish when his horse bucks at the edge. The scene from my earlier fantasy comes to life. However, the real Ikshu lifts his hat and waves it in my direction. He is a gentleman, my heart decides.

I wave my arm wildly to broadcast across the

distance, dislodging my ankle's hold on the branch. My serene lady pose turns to a fight for purchase, and I am thrown by my uncoordinated movements. Wiping the dust from my face, I lay prostrate on the ground. My book digs into the soft tissue beneath my corset. I spit grass from between my teeth. *Gross*.

There are a few small mercies. Ikshu is gone, so he didn't see my folly and his cuff is not harmed due to its wrapping in the blanket. I guess I got exactly what I deserved. As much as I love having my head in the clouds, the universe reminds me to keep my feet on the ground (literally) before I lead myself into greater danger.

Chapter 4

"No."

If he weren't twice my size and the center of my world, I would deck my brother. I hate that we are having this argument standing in front of my teepee, because he is taller than I am. I should be looking at him eye to eye, not craning upward as if he is Chebbeniathan, our Creator, come to life. "With one side of your mouth, you ask me to protect Olive and then deny me the rite of passage to manhood with the other. The rings tattooed on your chest represent the ability to look after a wife because you have proven yourself worthy. I am at the age you were when you received them. What is so wrong with the marching of time, Nartan?"

"I promise to bring back bundles of bones, beads, and porcupine quills if you stop whining and do this. I need your word you will watch over Olive and keep her from risking the babies with her wild behavior. My only hope is to find Sorrel Horse or another medicine man on the reservation to tell me how to help her when she goes into labor. Does she need to be in a bear or human form? Will she have babies or cubs? The most terrifying part is she doesn't have these answers either."

With every word, my brother stomps an intricate pattern in the dirt. He paces like the wolves along the fence line of our sheep enclosure. I've never seen him so agitated. It is as if the man who commands respect on both our earthen and the spiritual planes is afraid. Even when we were cast out of the Antelope Bend after the massacre and left to not only fend for ourselves but to keep our culture, Nartan never looked scared.

He selected our land and started to build our teepee. Then we built the vats, the frames, and smokehouses for tanning. While neither of us is a master carpenter, we built our barn with our hands. We learned to perfect woodworking before building an outhouse and cabin for Olive. One piece at a time, Nartan built our survival because he said it was so, and destiny listens to Nartan.

"Why would you leave the love of your life under the protection of a child?"

"You know I don't see you as a child—"

"You do, or there wouldn't be a problem."

"Look Ikshu. It's not you and stop rolling your eyes. The rings are tattooed after you earn your feathers. What are your deeds of bravery where you were given feathers in the sacred rite?"

"Well, let's see. Let's list them, Nartan." My voice reaches a volume it hasn't climbed to since we were children. Nartan's eyes boil at my tirade, but I'm only beginning. "All buffalo hunts are declared illegal by the US Government. All sacred ceremonies are banned as well as tribal gatherings on the reservations. How about I go to war with a rival tribe? Oh yes, I would die because we are a band of three members! Nartan, you can't depend on a system we aren't a part of anymore! I'm forever trapped as a boy in a man's body because the eagle feathers are no longer ours to bestow! I remain a child until our sacred rituals are restored!"

Nartan sighs and throws his hat in the dirt. His braids have become unraveled with the day's labors, and his eagle feathers are broken from being crushed into a hat daily. His hands smooth down his face repeatedly as if to stretch the lines of age and worry from it. It's not fair to dump this on him, but he, as a medicine man, has the tools to give me my rings. I have leaned on his strength my entire life, and maybe that is the root of the problem.

"Perhaps I should go to the reservation. I could bring back a note from Sorrel Horse with solutions to both our problems," I offer in peace.

"I couldn't torture you, Ikshu. Are you still awake half the night, or do you stay in the nightmares? I hear your screams, so don't deny them."

"Since the nightmares still haunt me, then it shouldn't matter if I go back there."

"You would have to travel through our bend's final circle area to get to the reservation and then face the people who survived with you. Finally, you would have to suck down your trauma to communicate with the elders until you got answers. Olive needs those answers. She needs her man to retrieve them. It is not that I don't think you could do it…eventually."

"A man's job and not a boy's, right?"

"I didn't mean to call you a boy…again."

"If we had stayed, I would be in the Tomahawk Lodge. You would either be with the medicine men or beside me in the lodge. In either case, we would be equals in the tribe. I would have a wife or maybe even two."

"Do you really believe that? With your handicrafts, they would have let you into the Lodge of the Braves? Only my fists kept them from beating you daily, and they still got to you behind my back. As you are now, they would have put you in the Spear Lodge. Don't try to deny it."

"I wouldn't be placed in the Spear Lodge because I'm firm of mind and body. Instead, my brother denies me the rites of passage, trapping me as his little pet. I'm not your son, Nartan! I'm your brother!"

"I don't think of you as my son. You just aren't a man. You are…you are…"

"Oh then, did you mean *Haxu'xan*?"

"Ikshu, I have never treated you as the third gender, and I never will."

"At one point, I thought I might be Haxu'xan because of your treatment of me. As a Shaman, you would be able to recognize the extra spiritual connection needed. I was relieved when I never developed powers like yours, because I could be just a man. All I want is to be a craftsman, a husband, and a father—not a mystic. Can you help me find my whole self? I don't have the spiritual powers to match you and probably never will. That is why my life sits in your palms."

"Ikshu, you aren't less than me."

"We both know your thoughts match your actions because you are pure of spirit. Your ability to call in a team of Water-Pouring Men at will is proof. You may say we are equals, but the thought of superiority must be there. Save the lies for someone who will believe them. Forget it, Nartan. I will guard our home from my humble position while you do what you do best."

"What's that?"

"Run to the spirit plane to hide in ceremonies and quests when the going gets tough." The fire has left my spirit, and my voice has cooled. I haven't just said my piece but thrown the whole pie at my brother. Nothing has changed. What's worse is Nartan's arguments make sense.

I want him to push me through a disappearing system. I squandered my chance when we were immersed in it. I was just a kid. How was I to know my world would come crashing down and my insides would rot with the horrors I would be forced to witness?

After a few laps around his woven path, Nartan raises his arms to the sky. He continues to stomp but now mumbles in our old language to beings I cannot see. I shake my head and shuffle my feet, so I don't gape like a fish at him. Having a Shaman for a brother should have brought me to expect these behaviors. Nothing can hold a candle to the strangeness of Nartan—except for maybe his wife. If only he could see himself, I chuckle to myself.

"Look, Ikshu. There must be a civilized way we can resolve this. The leaders are counting on us to make a new path for our people with the settlers. My guides indicate you need a new path to bravery. Your path will fit with our new life and circle."

"Your guides indicate?" My words drip with skepticism, and my brow tugs at the muscles in my forehead. Since when does Nartan listen to anyone on this plane, or the next?

"I want Olive out of danger, and you need danger to prove bravery. I propose a trade. Get her involvement in your business to zero. You make the deliveries. You broker the deals. With the tanning vats freezing overnight, we cannot treat hides until there is a break in the weather. You must be the face in town until the babies are old enough to let Olive travel once in a while. If you are brave enough to take over, you are brave enough for rings."

I stare at my brother as if he has grown two heads. Become a bona fide merchant? He might as well have asked me to knit wings and fly to the moon. I study his feathers and try to remember how he got them. It wasn't being pleasant and social, that's for sure. One was for his first Sun Dance. I visited Nartan while he hung from hooks until his flesh gave out and he received guidance. No thanks. Plus, I wouldn't know what visions to ask to receive. I don't need to know the future when Nartan is determined to make my every day the same.

Nartan's second feather came from avenging our mother when our father failed to come home. I was too young to remember but the story is a legend. They say Nartan ripped apart a man twice his size who tried to claim our mother while she was still in mourning. After seeing his ferocious side, no one messed with my brother or me. His third feather came from an event much less extraordinary. He went hunting. He brought home a buffalo. End of story. Why can't I have a mundane story?

I nod to Nartan because he expects an answer, and I don't have the words to fight. As much as I have longed for a business doing what I love, it hangs from my neck like a lead weight. Nartan is right, *sigh.* Nartan is always right. My mind wanders to thoughts of town while I stare at my boots and Nartan walks away. I talked to Cyrus at the party. I can visit him first.

I also talked to Ava at the party. What would she do if I visited her? Visions of her perched in a tree like a golden finch cloud my brain. She wore the boots I made, and I hope they kept her warm. The way she ran her fingers over my arm wheel showed her appreciation for its beauty. Did she realize I made it too? If she's agreeable to my presents, I could surround her with pretty things.

Would she give me a chance when we come from different worlds? Perhaps Nartan's challenge is just what I need to take the next step, not on his path but my own...a path into Wylder society and to the side of Miss Ava. Come to think of it, who was the elder man at her side? Obviously, her father, but which tribe is hers? She is Miss Ava...what?

Chapter 5

"Ava Wylder, you claim to be here to help out, but the gloves you left on the porch railing say the opposite," Finn yells from the doorway. His sentence is punctuated with the slam of the door behind him. He runs his hand through his shaggy hair with exasperation at me. My eldest brother lives next door so he can watch over us like a hawk. He may have moved out physically, but mentally he's managing more than the Wylder Store.

"We were just having coffee until you and Fletcher arrived," I snap at my grouchy brother. As we exit the house, I slam the door after my father, who knows to stay silent. Stepping onto the back porch, the storm cloud of masculine authority threatens to blot out the sunny yellow morning.

This was supposed to be a cheerful lunch to celebrate my homecoming. I'm just about to give my brother the business for assuming the worst of me when he drapes the gloves over my arm.

They aren't mine, or I didn't own them until now. I school my face before its smile shines brighter than the sun. The gloves are sheepskin with rabbit fur cuffs to match the boots from my admirer. Well, Ikshu hasn't admitted to making me gifts unless you count the beaded arm wheel I'm proudly wearing as a collar today.

I turn toward the porch railing to put my back to the men. They would find it strange that I am thrilled by my own gloves. But oh, I can't resist the furry interior sliding against my skin like a thousand little fingers caressing me.

"Thank you for retrieving them, Finn," I say sweetly, turning to face them. "I have been busy taking care of Dad, the house, and getting settled. I must have dropped them. I want Dad to be as comfortable as possible while lightening your load for as long as I am allowed to stay." I punctuate the statement with my sweetest smile.

Finn narrows his brown eyes at me and grinds his teeth in frustration. Dad's eyes bounce between us, but he stays out of our passive-aggressive confrontation. I love my brother, and he loves me in the way of siblings who are too alike for their own good. Our screaming matches are legendary.

Dad never wanted to show favoritism so he would take a step back when we butted heads. It was only when Abigail would intervene that we would retreat. With my sister staying with family in England, it is up to us to keep the peace and, most importantly, my chance to show him I'm an adult.

"You may want to slow down, Finn. Your strides are three times larger than mine. I can't wait to taste Jake and Elsie's biscuits either, but I doubt they will run out in the time it takes us to walk there. The bakers in New York use the same ingredients, but they aren't as good without a little love cut into the butter. Any news on Fletcher? I haven't seen him since Christmas."

"He will be here, Ava. He's got a lot on his shoulders for such a youngster." Dad's face is one of compassion while Finn looks like the top of his head is about to blow off. Is Finn fighting with everyone, or has

Dad's comment on responsibility touched a nerve? This is the opportunity I need! If I can convince Finn, I'm on his side—for once—he will convince Dad to let me stay on my behalf. This will free my time for adventure without the burden of returning to school hanging around my neck.

"Actually, he won't, Dad. He's meeting us at the restaurant," Finn says while dodging the hanging laundry which flies like oversized flags behind the dress shop. "Fletcher had to meet a grain shipment at the train depot for the Feed & Seed. Until we get more local suppliers, he's stuck dealing with grain hoppers and railway men."

Honestly, the oasis behind our house where we played as kids has seen better days. The alley was the castle, haunted forest, and ancient cave of our pretend play. The dress shop laundry provided sails for our pirate ships and clouds for our fairylands with the miles of hanging petticoats. The smoke from the gunsmith's forging stove was our fearsome dragon. Now the Long Horn Saloon has moved in with their clientele.

Cyrus the gunsmith is a dear friend of Father's and tries to keep the riffraff out, but he is just one man. Would Ikshu help the washerwomen fend off the habitually hungover? He wouldn't fuss at them but move them like an invincible force of nature with bulging biceps. *Sigh.* As we walk past the smithy, I can't help but wonder about Ikshu's holsters.

I bet the front window is empty after watching the holsters opened as presents at the party. If I watch the store, I can intercept Ikshu's holster delivery. He obviously found me if he is the one who put the gloves on the porch, so now it is my turn to find him. I'm giddy with excitement as a scheme brews in my head.

Despite the warm sun heating the alley behind our home, I wear my new gloves. The silky fur hugs my fingers as if their craftsman holds my hands. *Decadent.* Staring at my gloves causes me to stumble over a man laying across our path to the restaurant. Father catches my elbow before I can scuff my boots. Not even the morning-after-vomit of the straggler behind the Long Horn Saloon can dampen my spirits. I hope Father and Finn do not cause a scene by throwing him into the street in front of Jake's restaurant. The man is doubled over and moaning as if impaled on his own sword. I doubt he has the strength to cause mischief.

"Someone needs to do something about the behavior of these drifters," Finn grumbles as we approach Sidewinder Lane.

"Like what? The saloon offers rooms but cannot force men to buy them. No one wants to fuss with a drunk when they can throw them into the alley."

"Yes, but the alley leads to our back porch. Perhaps we should brick the door into a wall. I don't like them having such easy access to you when I'm not at home. Having Ava staying with you is like dangling a carrot in front of a mule's nose. A break-in is bound to happen," Finn grouses.

Finn needs to stop filling Dad's head with imaginary dangers, or my plans will go up in smoke. My presence cannot be seen as a liability. Filling in the back door will eliminate my means of secret escape for our front door opens beneath the windows of Finn's apartments over the Wylder Store.

"The Wylder Family Home has stood proudly longer than the saloons, the shops, and the town itself. It will not be breached so easily by the clumsy hands of a drunken scoundrel." My words belt out with more vinegar than I intend and earn raised eyebrows from both men.

"I bet you would like to have running water in the kitchen, Ava. Some of Fletcher's boys could install a sink with taps when they close the wall." Dad's loving suggestion gives me pause. If I act excited about having a sink, then I'm positioning myself as mistress of the house and a permanent resident. However, I will be a permanent resident without a clean means of escaping. I gaze lovingly at my new gloves and the toes of my new boots which peek out of the hem of my dress with each step.

Could I use the more brazen way to sneak off and see Ikshu, or should I test the waters with Dad on my secret crush? Such thoughts are premature outside of my novels as Ikshu hasn't said a positive word in my direction. However, the loving hug on my calves with each step tells the opposite tale. The only certainty is I have fallen in love with his craftsmanship.

The gifts may be a ploy to make his goods into a fashion trend. What better way to advertise your business than to have Ava Wylder strutting around town wearing your finery? I hate playing the pawn, but Ikshu struck me as genuine. I have been spending too much time with two-faced scoundrels disguised as gentlemen. Lumping him in the same category churns my stomach and steals my appetite.

"Watch it, Ava." Finn grabs my shoulders at the end of the ally. I narrowly escaped being plowed under by a buggy full of giggling ladies. In my bitter thoughts, I walked into traffic without looking. "You were nearly trampled. Why did you keep walking when we stopped five paces behind you? Where is your head?"

"I'm sorry, Finn. I was dreaming of a new sink." I swing my eyes to him and pour syrup over my tone of voice. At school, it made any man eat out of my hand. I get a suspicious side-eye from my brother. He suspects I'm up to something, but how bad could it be that I plan to stay home? It's not like I'm running off with a tribe to live in the wild. *Scheez.*

"It's safe to cross. Let's shake a leg kids," Dad says to quell a brewing storm more than to hurry us along. He puts his arm around my shoulders, and I pat his hand as we cross. Instead of the warmth of love, I get a rock of guilt on my chest. Admonishments of my New York chaperones fill my head with threats to tell my father the trouble I caused at school. I may have hidden my cigars, but I could never get the smell out of my clothes. I laughed off each time I was caught playing cards with the maids, but with my dad smiling down at me now, it is not so funny.

We haven't entered the restaurant, and the noise is pricking at my nerves as if I'm resting on a bed of nails. I lean my head on Dad's shoulder to plug one ear against the onslaught. *Thud!* The bottom step of Jake's slams against my shin as I forget to step onto it.

The noise turns the heads of those waiting to enter the restaurant and my companions. If it weren't for my thick boot cuffs reaching my knees, I would be howling in pain. Ikshu has managed to keep me safe without smothering me which is an art I wish my family would learn.

"Ava, watch out, again. What is wrong with you? Did you forget to watch where you are going in your highfalutin schooling?" My brother blasts at me in front of half of Wylder and I shrink with mortification. My shoulders curl into their habitual protective position.

Everyone stares. We are the Wylder family, so the all-seeing eyes of gossip are a natural part of our lives. Diners from inside crane their necks to see who is getting the business end of my brother. My shoulders curl tighter, and my arms cross my middle in an instinctive posture to guard my tender innards.

More criticism from my New York tutors flood into my brain—they hated when I crossed my arms. Women should be open, friendly, and with graceful posture. I'm none of those things and struggle to pull off the act.

"Are you hurt, honey?"

"No, Dad, only my ego is bruised. Let's set me in a chair before I do some real damage." I flash a self-deprecating smile to my dad. When we had moments like this in my childhood, he would have carried me into the restaurant. The expression on his face indicates he is having the same flashback to those days as me. We compromise by walking into Jake's with his arm around my shoulders, following the tempting smell of gravy.

Fletcher is seated at a large table in the center of the room. He waves us over, and my brothers exchange smiles. The heavy rock in my stomach drops behind my belly button. *Great*. The whole town will have the perfect view of our conversation.

The clinking of cutlery on plates slows as we pass each table. Everyone greets my father, but I only receive critical perusal from head to toe. Just like in New York, I long for a life where I'm not a doll on a shelf. After my brothers shake hands, Finn pulls out my chair as if our spat outside never happened.

Oh, how I wish I could run into the wilderness and live authentically! I could create a simple life of quiet honesty without societal pressures. I would dance among the trees and woodland animals in a dress made of leaves, like a nymph. I would be one with…Ikshu steps into my forest fantasy and being dressed in leaves goes from being spiritual to indecent.

I scan the restaurant with flushed cheeks as if the diners can see inside my head. *How silly!* They are looking for scandal, and luckily they aren't able to find it inside my mind.

"Ava, what's around your neck? Some fashion from the Old States, or has a husband finally yoked you?" Fletcher grins at me with cheeks full of biscuit mush. When were they delivered, or were they on the table when we arrived? I wish I had the ladylike ability to filter out the people staring and focus on enjoying my life.

"Hardy har, har," I grouse in return. "This collar is Wylder fashion. I have a secret admirer who has been leaving me gifts." As in my admirer is a secret from you until I can have a conversation with him.

"What is it?" Finn leans closer, and I let him inspect the collar.

"It is beadwork in the shape of some bird, I think. I liked how it matched my dress, so I wore it," I lie with a shrug. The orange phoenix rising from the graying bone beads is stunning. I spent an hour trying to decide if my scarlet dress or my matching gray dress best offset the piece.

The decisions came after a late night drawing it in my journal and writing a short story about the bird. I burnt an entire candle while obsessing over the time and care that went into making it. The gray beads were once ivory ones but have accumulated a layer of wear to them. They must have rubbed against Ikshu's arm for years. The same cuff rests upon the bare skin of my neck, so I can imagine the sensation of Ikshu's hand on me.

"I've seen this symbol before, but I can't place it," Finn says to Fletcher.

"I know," Fletcher agrees. "If it's a local guy, I'm sure he's visited the store as well as the feed depot. We will have to keep an eye out for who is trying to court our little sister. Ava, why didn't you bring a Yankee home to scare off the Wylder ruffians?"

"Because my head wasn't turned by any of the Yankees, Fletcher. You would have been appalled. Blowhard boys calling themselves men when they didn't know the first thing about caring for their horses. Imagine the carelessness. They would leave their horses saddled after riding and look at me as if I had grown two heads when I asked about brushing. Don't get me started on their shiny boots which had never seen dirt or their puffed sleeves which had never been rolled for working."

"I'm sure you put them to rights," Finn says with a mischievous smile to Fletcher. They share a knowing glance at my expense, but for once, I don't take the bait.

"No, I wasn't to speak on such things. It isn't ladylike to have knowledge of horses, working, or anything not involving babies."

"If someone mistreated an animal, your mother's fuse would be lit. If they tried to silence her objections to it, watch out! Her powder keg would blow."

"Well, at least we know where Ava gets it." This time, my treacherous father joins in on the laughter.

"Mom loved Wylder too. She belonged in the

wilderness. That's why you brought her here. Right, Dad?"

"Not exactly. We hopped on the first train west after we eloped. Your wild mother climbed up my parent's house and proposed through the window. I was so smitten, I followed her to the preacher in the dead of night. You got your love of climbing trees from her as well."

"Being in New York, it was obvious I am a western girl. Climbing trees, speaking your mind, caring for horses are all things frowned upon for young ladies. I was lucky they let me ride, but then again it was only for courting outings with a chaperone. Where is the fun in exploring with an entourage?"

"I'm glad you did a little riding while you were away. I remember how you cried when leaving Lady," Dad says tenderly.

"Only once or twice. New York doesn't have the space for leisurely riding."

"But they have excitement filling those spaces, right?"

"I guess," I say with a sigh.

We pause to order the afternoon special of meatloaf with mashed root vegetables smothered in gravy. I struggle to focus on the waitress with all the conversations swarming around my head like bees. I hear my name at other tables and realize they aren't talking to me but about me. In New York, it was no better. I wasn't the subject of conversation because of my name but my clothes, accent, poor posture, and shrew reputation.

"You were so excited to see the museum. What happened?" Fletcher asks when the waitress disappears to fill our mineral water glasses.

"I saw them. That's all. A new exhibit comes through once every few years, so it is not new."

"I'm sure the company you held made each visit fresh and exciting." The expectations in Dad's eyes threaten to break my spirit. I have failed him in every way. I can only hope Abigail's tenure in England is making up for my shortcomings as a daughter.

"If you like fairy tales perhaps," I say with more acid than a lemon. "I struggled to find someone who didn't have a war story that grew with every telling. I got to hear three or four versions of the same story in a single turn about the museum."

"Ava, men's lives were changed forever by the war. You can't blame them for being torn by combat," Finn says before snatching the last biscuit from the basket.

"That's the problem, though. My suitors are in their mid-twenties at best, so when the war began, they were toddlers. I refuse to play dumb. Did they really expect me to believe they shot down legions and wrestled adult soldiers in hand-to-hand combat in their nappies?" My brothers chuckle. Dad mops his brow with his napkin to hide his expression.

"You could have used their companionship to go to the theater, opera, or musical performances, right?"

"Dad, I can't tolerate the noise at the outdoor Wylder theater. How long do you think I lasted in an opera house filled with people listening to sopranos? Not to the first intermission if you are trying to guess. I pretended to faint just so I could be carried out instead of fighting through the rows."

"No, Ava, you didn't." Fletcher's eyes are round with embarrassment on my behalf. We take turns leaning back so our meals can be placed before us.

"Yes, and worse to retreat to somewhere quiet. I would do anything to avoid going back to the city." Being too slow to grab biscuits, I tuck in at once. I have the first meaty cube before my lips in seconds.

"Oh really," Finn says in his suspicious tone. The laughter has fled for the hills from his voice. He puts Fletcher on high alert. The men stare at me. The restaurant quiets as if everyone has stopped chatting to stare at me.

I've already dug my hole so I might as well jump in. "I want to stay in Wylder not only to help Dad take care of our home but write a cowboy novel with authentic cowboys." I hardly get the words out before Fletcher bursts into giggles. Dad's frown is more puzzlement than anger. Finn's grip on his glass threatens to smash it into a thousand pieces.

"Oh, you had me there for a minute, Ava," Fletcher says, pretending to wipe tears from his eyes.

"Do you have the commitment to write an entire book, honey? You were never the type of girl to cross-stitch a pillowcase or knit a scarf. You claimed boredom and would run outside." My brothers nod in agreement with my father and my temperature rises.

"I read books cover to cover." I wish my voice sounded more strong than whiny. "Writing is different from handicrafts because I love words, not things." Well, usually I don't love things. I have been fixated on my gifts from Ikshu. Maybe I should give myself more credit and say I'm fixated on the man, not the things. On second thought, that line of thinking is less virtuous than simply being shallow.

"I'm sure you would write an exciting book, but why here? You can write anywhere. Being in New York gives you more experiences and people to write about. I would hate for you to end up a spinster on a foolish whim." Finn's words make sense but steal my appetite. I was sent to New York to find a husband to take care of me not better myself. Little Ava is out of sight, out of mind.

"I certainly do not want to end up a spinster," I concede.

"You're as beautiful as your mother, inside and out. The appropriate man will come along when you least expect it. I would hate for you to miss him because you are on the wrong end of the railway line."

Oh, Dad, I have the same fear. If I'm surrounded by lily-fair sissies, I will miss the romance I crave. How do I tell them what I want is on this end of the railway line? I don't plan on being a spinster or a kept lady in a manor. I will be a frontier wife on an adventure with my true love, whether they approve or not. How can my family be disappointed when I want exactly what Mom and Dad had?

Chapter 6

Why couldn't wrapping oneself in a blanket and staring at a fire be the way to spiritual enlightenment? I can no longer feel my toes and question the sanity of going on a vision quest in late December. Nartan, the expert on vision quests, gave me two days to meditate in the wilderness before he needs me to watch over our homestead. When did he ever have a deadline for communing with the spiritual plane?

I settle my rising temper with a deep breath. The frigid air burns my nose, stings my chest, and cools my spirit. Last night, I traveled to Medicine Bow Mountain instead of my usual wandering around the homestead. I rarely sleep more than a few hours at a time before the nightmares find me. I walked south until the homesteads grew further apart, the forest thinned, and the landscape changed from flat to hills. Under the light of the moon, I followed the majestic mountain's shadow in the hopes of delivering my soul from darkness.

I will not make the same mistake as Nartan and leave our circle unattended. I cannot justly blame him for what happened all those years ago, but somehow, I still do. Perhaps that is why I haven't connected to a spirit team or even a teacher. It is not residual fear from the incident but residual anger with no proper outlet. Nartan left me alone when he was all I had. He set the boundary of putting himself first without explanation or apology.

He continues to do so but asks me to compromise my journey. If only he wasn't a hypocrite, I wouldn't be seeing red.

"I release the anger toward my brother for choosing his spiritual health over mine so I can move forward with the progression of my spiritual journey." My words echo over the rolling hills beneath my perch on a cliffside of Medicine Bow Mountain. A hawk cries in the distance as Mother Earth acknowledges my plea. The sunrise chases the shadows up my body, then from my face, and finally out of the crown of my head. The loving light of nature burns the pain, fear, anger, and resentment from my spirit.

The blinding low winter sun cleanses my past, shines on my present, but only hints to my future. I breathe in unison with the Earth. I am free. With my newly polished soul, I wait for messages. After a few hours, my limbs tremble with cold like a shaky engine fighting for fuel. I curl myself tightly into a ball for warmth. Is this smart? Doubts threaten to destroy the meditative state I have worked so hard to achieve. My ego swirls nasty internal messages until I have worked my temper into an angry swarm of bees.

To add insult to injury, the buffalo herd migrates over the hills below. From this height, they are small slow dots rearranging themselves into shapes like grains of sand. Nartan's words echo in my head. He's saying, "Hunt the buffalo to get the feathers, then present your feathers to the elders to make the case for tattoo rings." My brother grows from man to monster in my mind's eye. In his backhanded humble way, he puts himself as the elder of our mini tribe with the power to decide my fate. Having a medicine man for a big brother is a blessing and a curse.

"Can you please talk to me? How can I know what to do to make you happy when you don't communicate with me?" It is time to cut the middleman out from between my existence and the spiritual plane. I throw a rock over the cliffside in frustration. Clouds of air puff from my nostrils as the bull inside me rages.

Gentle snowflakes begin to fall. Not enough to cover the ground or be seen from afar, but enough to distract me from my diatribe. My mind settles as each flake finds a home on my tunic.

"You've said your lesson with silence, haven't you," I say with dry laughter and a palm against my face. "I'm not getting what I want because I am not adequately communicating. I am frustrating those around me with my half-stated demands laced with fear." Mother Earth works in mysterious ways, but she's always right. My eye roll brings my face toward the heavens where little stings of snowflakes remind me of the tough love I am receiving. I cannot move forward with my life without learning to communicate. It is not just talking but exchanging information.

With a steam-filled sigh, I collapse onto my back. I throw my arms and head onto the ground in surrender. *Ouch!* My offering must have been rejected because a rock stabs at the back of my skull. Really, what was that for? I roll over to dig out the offending stone with my nails. We will see who is boss when I hurl it off the cliffside.

The rock is a nearly translucent blue stone with glittering pieces of gold woven through it. Cordierite. I roll the palm-sized gem in my hands. Golden-colored versions of this stone were collected only to be rejected when the settlers first came here to look for real gold.

They traded cordierite to our tribal circle in exchange for food when their ignorance drove them to starvation. As a kid, I loved this stone for the blue shadows it cast in the afternoon sun. Nartan loved them too, for they are used in healing illnesses of the spirit. They increase willpower but do more…oh what was it?

Sleep.

Cordierite increases the individual's power over their ability to sleep peacefully. Mother Earth supplies everything we need if we are patient. Message received. Does this crystal have the power to stop the nightmares? Can it erase the story written on the backs of my eyelids? The memory of the massacre plays out night after night. I was sitting in Grandmother Winter's teepee while she teaches me to tuft brushes. She had her back to the door.

When the white man's hand came through the canvas, he snatched her. It could have easily been me. While her screams filled my ears, I crawled out the back of the teepee and tore off into the forest. I outran the horses who were circling the village. I climbed the tallest tree I could find to wait for Nartan. My heart hammered in my ears for three days.

Despite my blessings, the hand reaches into my dreams and jerks me from safety. Awake I am grown but asleep, I am a little boy crawling under the canvas. With the help of Mother Earth, I may find solace in sleep again. I have a home, a business, a precious gift, and all I need to move to the next phase of my life if I am willing to wait. Nartan waited, and he received Olive. The love shining between them is blinding and will bless our home with children in the spring. Is a similar dream worth the wait?

Ava's voice floats through my mind. "Merry Christmas, Ikshu."

Has she ever danced in the blue shadows cast from cordierite in the afternoon sun? I wonder if she sleeps soundly. Does she dream of a family? Has she ever looked at a man with eyes filled with love? I examine the stone for the message of whether she would ever gaze in my direction as a wife looks to her husband. Does she need this crystal more than I?

The rock doesn't speak to me, but it will. My face pulls with the joy of divine inspiration. I will make an ornament with this gift. I will give it to her with the instructions to place it in her window if she is willing to give me a chance. I will need porcupine quills and horsehair for weaving but will make do with the beads I have. I can't wait until Nartan comes back with more supplies from the reservation I must know now.

I scramble from my position on the ground and jog toward home. My cold limbs protest but not as loudly as the plans forming in my head. FoolsGold is getting a haircut. I will weave the most intricate design of my career. Finally, I need to convince Olive to write the note without giving away my plans. Thank you for the inspiration, Mother Earth, even if I still have no guides or teachers. You may not give me what I want, but you always supply what I need.

Chapter 7

He jumps astride his steed with his duster flying in the wind. He must race to his ladylove before she weds a scoundrel.

Well, that's the opposite of what I wanted to write. The more I scribble in my journal, the more ridiculous my hero's actions become. Not only would he injure himself if he jumped on a horse, but he would have to be nine feet tall to accomplish it. There is the added obstacle of the leather duster.

If it got tangled beneath him, it would pull on his shoulders. The horse would be startled by such reckless behavior as well. He would be grassed in seconds. My hero would be trampled in an instant, and his ladylove would be doomed to a loveless marriage. How's that for a happily ever after? *Sigh, being a novelist is more difficult than I thought.*

It is impossible in this parlor. Mom's taste in furniture was simple and locally made. The deep brown leather and woods are soothing. There is nothing wrong with the room itself, except for the fine layer of dust Father allows to grow on every surface. It is the noise from the street outside through our closed windows. Buggies squeaking, horses clomping, endless chatter, and even a gunshot crowd the space in my head. I slam my book closed and shake a fist at the window. The cotton curtains wave back at me as if I am dismissed. I stomp with ire upstairs to my room. At least the doilies dampen the noise.

No, lying is more difficult than the truth. I sigh at my book once I reach my room. My heart isn't into my story because the hero is all wrong for me. He's not the New York gentlemen with less fortitude than the paper he's written upon. However, he's got the colorful passion of the dull white linen. If I'm going to be a sensation in the world of American literature, I might as well throw all my chips in. I scribble over the bland words in my journal and replace them with the fantasy from my dreams.

"Come on, my dear friend. I need your help," he whispers to his trusted steed. He gently climbs astride, but man and beast are of one mind. Their hearts beat in unison. His braids pound his back like battle drums as the pair race toward the chapel. He must rescue his ladylove before she weds a cowboy when her heart is as wild as the hawk who flies over the prairie.

There. Perfect. Perfectly scandalous.

I lay my pen on the pages while rolling onto my back. The floor is colder than I remember. Would it be strange if my dad found me laying on the floor with my gloves on? I may not be the perfect daughter, but I have never done anything for him to doubt my sanity…that I didn't get away with. My thoughts drift from my father to Ikshu. What would he think of my schoolyard scandals? Would he laugh at my antics or think I am privileged and immature?

Enough with forcing a novel from my pen today or ever. Who am I kidding? My brothers nailed the issue at the restaurant. I'm better at reading than writing. I crawl to my bed and slide my Jules Verne book from the foot.

With a sigh of contentment, I stretch my cramped muscles.

Writing requires too much hunching over. If I met Jules Verne, would he have a hunchback from writing all his glorious adventures? I open my stolen book to my placeholder and Ikshu's note falls out. At least I hope the secret admirer note is from Ikshu.

The gift appeared on the porch yesterday. I walked all the way to the apothecary to get a special pie seasoning blend just to get some time alone to read the note. My errand also gave my father a logical story of origin for the ornament hanging in my window. I roped myself into making a pie, but the stirrings I feel when I look at the ornament are worth the extra cooking. With a smile reaching my eyes, I read the poem for the hundredth time:

Beauty is more than its blue hue.
It protects you while you sleep.
Hang it in your window with intentions true,
If it is me, you wish to keep.

From my star-shaped pose on the floor, I can watch the sun's rays bounce off my new window ornament. The packets of blue light dance around the ceiling with each shake of my head, calling laughter from my belly. How could a rock suspended from a braid of hair stir my emotions so?

It must be a magical crystal possessed with spirits from Ikshu's medicine man brother. What was his name again? I'm just grateful they bring spirits of joy instead of suffering. Knowing I could be ruined physically, socially, and spiritually add to Ikshu's mystique and allure. Before I found the gift on our porch, I had thought he had forgotten me.

Knock, knock. "Ava, may I come in?"

"Of course, Dad. I'm working on my novel, and I wanted to close out the noise of the town as much as possible," I call from my spot on the floor.

Dad steps through the door to sit at my pink frilly vanity. The weathered man looks ridiculous among the delicate lace. He earned every line and callous building Wylder from the ground up with Mom. They were alone against the wilderness. He steeples his fingers, and I know I'm in for it.

Dad never raised his voice at me but instead drones on in endless lectures. I sigh and sit up against the chest at the foot of the bed. I clutch my book to my chest. How would he react if he saw my infatuation with a Native in black and white?

"Ava," he starts on a whisper, "I have lived alone since your mother died, and I can take care of myself. I have done it successfully while you were in school—despite what Finn may have told you. I'm not losing my marbles, but I hear the rumors in town. I gave my wits temporarily to my grief, but now I have all my faculties back."

"Dad, I never said—" He raises his hand to stop me.

"I understand you want to do what's best for me. Princess, you are making a big mistake. Don't you see how a partnership with a family in the Old States would help our businesses? Don't you see how a visit with a wagon full of grandkids would lift my spirits? Don't you see how much we worry about you here? I was planning to spend the afternoon playing checkers and then an early supper with my friends. I was swamped with guilt when I smelled your pie."

"Never mind the pie. You can spend the day with

your friends. I will be here when you get back. I never meant to put you in a cage." The sincerity of my words stops his lecture. I let them hang between us with their emotional baggage left unsaid. Indeed, I never meant to imprison him because New York is my cage. He lowers his brow at me as the unsaid words sink in.

"There is a wide world out there waiting for you and the perfect partner to explore it. You cannot find your match sitting in this house. I will not let you waste away your youth. Since you have been home, you spend most of your days cooped up in your room."

"What if my match isn't in New York?" The words are whispered with caution. He will never accept anyone less than a gentleman…I think. He would be disappointed if he knew how much time I spent in the library in New York. Probably more disappointed than if he knew how much time I spent in the servant's quarters playing cards. "I'm busy in this room. I'm writing a novel."

His eyes swing to my scribbled notebook on the floor before revealing the pity in them to me. He doesn't believe in my project. He's humoring me to avoid my temper. The sting brings moisture to the corners of my eyes. "Ava, you can write anywhere, but the suitors aren't anywhere. They are in civilized cities not a town like Wylder."

"If living here is so horrible, why did you raise your family here? Why did you drag Mom here?"

"It wasn't me who did the dragging," he says with a sad smile. "Parents always want better for their children. The boys are happily running the stores, but I bet they would trade you spots in a heartbeat. You want adventure, so I provided it. Your adventure is in New

York."

"Isn't part of the adventure deciding your own fate?"

"Aren't you going to choose a husband who loves you and a house full of children? Come on, Ava. I know you want motherhood as much as Abigail. She is taking England by storm. Do you want to go to England too?"

"Oh no," I say with vigorous headshakes. "England is laced tighter than New York. I want to be free, Dad."

"Of all my children, you are most like your mother." He wipes his hand down his face. "She found freedom in me, I guess. We set off on a grand adventure together—"

"You gave her everything. Why can't I have it all too?"

"You can and more with the opportunities in New York."

"I can't, Dad," I say more to my lap than his face. My posture curls into my trusted shelter. My shoulders roll in, and I stoop a few inches shorter. My arms cross to protect my middle. In New York, I would earn admonishment. "Will you give me winter term, if I promise to make social calls here?"

"There are no social calls here. People here are busy."

Because they have meaningful lives. "I won't get in your way. A few more weeks is all I'm asking."

"What are you going to find in a few weeks? What aren't you telling me?"

Ikshu's poem peeks at me from beneath my discarded book. I need to be more aggressive in my pursuit of him to see it through. I must find out if he lives up to my fantasy hero before I am swept away to the doldrums of New York. The sun is released from behind a cloud and throws blue dots around the room. I smile at the dot over my heart. Dad frowns at the window as if seeing the ornament for the first time.

"I picked it up at the apothecary when I went for pie spices. It is to help me sleep."

"You still have trouble sleeping?"

"It is worse in New York. The traffic never stops, and the voices on the street keep me awake."

"More than the ones from Long Horn?"

"Much more. In Wylder, I know I can find peace."

He raises an eyebrow at me as if he can read the words I have hidden between the lines. I sleep peacefully here because I am dreaming of a wild Arapaho man and our many adventures—a man my father would never approve of and who has the power to blow the tops of my brothers' heads off just by standing at my side. I love to play with fire, but will my obsession with Ikshu blast me back to New York like a cannonball?

What if he is less than my dreams have painted him to be? The sand is draining from my hourglass faster than Ikshu is taking this courtship. Why isn't Ikshu asking me to stroll along Buckboard Alley? If it weren't for his gifts, I would say our relationship is completely one-sided. It's funny I spend most of my time running from conversations with suitors. Now that I have found one to interest me, he is nowhere to be found. Does he appeal to me because of the danger, the taboo, or because he simply hasn't ruined it by opening his mouth?

Chapter 8

A whole week to myself. Nartan's trip to the Wind River reservation has opened my eyes to how my brother's presence puts me out of sorts. I had the most serene meditation as he left. My lungs can expand fully without the weight of my brother's expectations suffocating me. I hardly noticed the cold nipping at my face. He plans to be back by nightfall, but there is no way. Even Olive rolled her eyes at his blubbering when he left. It will take four days of spiritual dances to get past the initiation of the Dog Lodge, assuming they will admit him. The Dog Lodge holds the spiritual leaders from all the bends. Nartan, as a medicine man, should fit in, but they may reject him for living in Wylder.

Our tanning business is at a standstill too. The vats were emptied before Mother Earth could freeze them solid. It isn't worth rebuilding a busted vat to tan the few skins we get in the winter. The cows who die this time of year are diseased with mangy hides. We take pride in the quality of our rawhide and treated leather. I thought to spend the day hunting rabbits for boots and tobacco pouches. However, my sister-in-law wanted to get one last hunt before Nartan left. I received the skins of her labor. Nartan had roasted rabbit before he left, and hopefully the stew Olive is making for supper doesn't kill us. She tries, but I wish she wouldn't.

When I return to my teepee, my mind wanders to

Ava. Did she hang the cordierite charm in her window? Is she waiting for me to visit? Fantasies of her exploding from the doors of her stately home to launch herself into my arms warm my heart. She would then introduce me to her family. I would move into the Wylder house until we bought our own little house in town.

We would wed with Nartan and Olive in the audience…or would Nartan preside? Would they feel abandoned if I left? Could they do it alone? My dream turns into a nightmare. Olive doesn't know how to garden, and Nartan hasn't the patience for it. With the babies to raise, the homestead would be too much. The beautiful cabin he built would fall into disrepair. Miniature Nartans would run through the streets of Wylder begging for food.

Ah! I have to stop before this mess manifests!

I hold my ears and squat to the floor of my teepee. My forehead rests on the buffalo skin as I breathe in the scent of the treated hide. The nightmare clears. If Ava is the one for me, she would live on the Sagebrush Homestead. Even without the comparison to the stately home she currently lives inside, my teepee looks shabby. If I stretched out on the floor, my height would span the diameter. Supplies for my art litter the edges while a pile of completed wares guards the entrance.

At least the layers of inviting bearskins would keep her warm at night while I roamed to distance myself from my night terrors. The canvas is sturdy and warded with Nartan's symbols. This was the first structure on our homestead and where we both slept until a year ago. Nartan got it into his head to have a wife and built her a cabin with his hands. I helped a little but not as much as I should have.

Is living in this tiny structure asking too much in exchange for a broken man like me? I have nothing else to offer her. I would know if I checked her window. A hanging amulet on the glass would mean a fair shake while an empty window means I should give up on marrying a lady so highfalutin. My inner self encourages me to build a cabin for her next to Olive's. If Ava is a better cook than Olive, Nartan would help me build it too.

We could be happy on this land if Ava gave me a chance. At the foot of the bed, which I use as a couch during the day, there's a pile of holsters. I could take those to Cyrus whose shop is under her window. I would have my answer and a step toward owning my business. I talked to him once. I can do it again...for Ava.

A few hours later, FoolsGold sniffles and bucks toward the water trough in front of the gunsmith. I stand frozen in the road. Blue shadows ring the window at the top right of Ava's house. I lead FoolsGold toward the window and away from his goal. The horse neighs in protest but follows my lead. Are my eyes playing tricks on me? In the window hangs the ornament I made. Our game has progressed to my turn. If she can take the leap of faith by putting an Arapaho symbol in her window, I can sell my holsters to Cyrus.

I tie FoolsGold next to the trough. The greedy splash of the horse mists my back with water as I stand before the door. *Inhale.* One step. *Exhale.* Two steps. My pulse thunders in my ears. Shallow breaths lift my chest in rapid succession, clinking the beads on my apron. I push the bag of holsters onto them to dampen the noise. *Calm wind, please fill my chest, and fortify my spirit.* The gentle prayer flows from my mind through my body and grounding into the earth below my feet. I open the door.

Thank goodness there are no customers. The left wall is covered with guns, yoked by chains like beads on a string. I suppose having them locked is best, but the display reminds me of a cross between an evil charm bracelet and a firing squad. Only slightly less frightening is the forge hearth at the back of the shop. Flames leap within its cavernous mouth as it awaits its next meal like the Hiintcabiit monster of the rivers. Only true respect will keep the beast from feeding upon the humans with the courage to work with them. While I love my art, I doubt my constitution could handle working in an area surrounded by instruments of death like Cyrus. He is the blend of brave and craftsman I aspire to be.

"Ikshu, what a pleasant surprise," Cyrus calls from behind his workbench. Pieces of a long-barreled shotgun and tools I've never seen before litter the table before him. I nod with a broad smile and advance to his outstretched hand. "Is your bag full of holsters? I have had a few requests for black ones. I guess you cannot get black ones in Cheyenne, so all manner of ruffians are visiting Wylder."

"Olive mentioned your request. I have eight black holsters, four of each size, as well as seven rawhide ones. I have matching belts for the four smaller black holsters too." My words are just above a whisper. Cyrus leans toward me to hear. Instead of being embarrassed over my volume, I'm grateful the words came out at all.

"That's mighty fine. This has turned into a profitable friendship. I love the business, even if it is bringing strangers to these parts. I guess having such a fine railway stop does that already."

"Yes, it does," I agree because I have no opinion on

the matter. The silence stretches awkwardly between us. Cyrus nods. I nod. His eyes bounce around as if physically looking for something to say to me. I want to say something too. More silence.

"If you want to put them in the window, I'll cash you out and let you on your way." Cyrus puts us out of our misery. He retreats to his safe in the corner of the shop while I walk to the opposite corner of the room to unload my bag at the window.

Whinny. I'm arranging holsters when FoolsGold's neigh catches my attention. A second Missouri Fox Trotter is taking up more than half of the water trough. A gloved hand lovingly pets his snout. I made those gloves. Her laughter carries from between the two horses. Then I see her…Ava.

Her hair is piled on her head like a feathered headdress from a golden eagle. Her eyes sparkle with mischief as she laughs in my direction. The melody stretches her lips over the shining pearls in her mouth. She captivates me. The delicate hand moves from FoolsGold to the base of her throat. She tips her head back, exposing her neck to me. As it undulates, I wonder if she is as soft as she looks.

Forcing my eyes to move from her throat to her dress is the biggest mistake I could make. The blue shiny material changes shade with every dip and curve of her figure. At the party, the large chair had acted as a shell while she curled into herself like a turtle. Shoulders slumped. Eyes suspicious. Lips firm. With the sunlight, she has emerged in all her beauty.

Her posture may have straightened, but her frame is slight as if she can't shoulder burdens on her own. The kind of woman who needs a pair of strong shoulders to block out the worst of life, and in return, she will provide grace, color, and poetry.

Any of the cowboys in Wylder could act as her haven. However, her crossing my path this time cannot be a coincidence. The blue ornament in her window is not happenstance either. Speaking of windows, I have no more reason to linger before this one. It is full of holsters, but I'm trapped either by her beauty or my shyness. If I move, will she disappear? She swings her gaze to meet mine. Like magic, the storm clouds within her eyes turn green. Perhaps she has bewitched me.

"Here's your payment, Ikshu." Cyrus's voice hammers through my skull. I jump two feet in the air, knocking holsters onto the floor.

"Thank you," I say, more to the holsters on the floor than the man. "I'll just get this put in order and ride on out of here."

"Only if she lets you."

"What do you mean?" Terror freezes my hands upon the holsters on the ground. Had I been caught staring? Is Ava someone special to Cyrus? My insides clench as I prepare myself for a warning or his backhand.

"Looks like Ava Wylder's horse has taken a shine to yours. Little Miss Wylder is just romantic enough to hold you hostage until the two lovebirds settle things."

"She's Ava…Wylder." The air rushes from my chest in a whoosh. Good thing I'm already crouched to the floor with my head between my knees. "Wylder as in the name of our town?"

"Yep, her parents built this place from the ground up. Wylder Mercantile, Wylder Feed & Seed, and the Wylder family home out back are owned by her father and brothers. They are a close-knit family."

"She's Ava Wylder," I whisper as I stand. I place the holsters on the windowsill while avoiding the scene through the glass. There must be some mistake. How could the Princess of Wylder have looked at me twice? How did I not ask her last name at the party? Dreams of being hers go up in smoke as the usual gray cloud of sadness forms in my mind. I can't lay a finger on Ava…Wylder.

Chapter 9

"FoolsGold doesn't usually like to share." The whisper of his voice dances over my shoulder and taps down my arm. Bent over the water trough, I miss his exit from the gunsmith and his approach behind me.

"That must be why he likes me. I don't share either," I flirt. Beneath my fluttering lashes, I leer at his face. He should be smiling. Instead, he looks like a mouse in an open field awaiting a hawk or owl to swoop down and devour him.

"I need him to take me home." As nervous as his tone is, the timbre rumbles with masculinity. He checks for prying eyes over his shoulder. It's adorable that he thinks he has a moment of privacy. Small shells clink together as the braids buried in his mass of hair swing. What if he is meeting someone here? Could he have a wife or, heaven forbid, multiple wives?

"Where is home?" Not knowing his marital status would cause a gentler woman to take caution. However, the desire to know everything about him overrides my common sense.

"Southwest, quite a distance outside of town. The Sagebrush Homestead is due south of the common green where the path intersects with the feeder stream to the Medicine Bow River."

"What's so interesting about home?" I lean against the horse in a pose I remember from an art museum. The painting looked scandalous, but I feel ridiculous. My tone is flirtatious, but inside my confidence falters. I made a lot of assumptions to get to this point. I assumed he made the leather gifts, the ornament, the poem that went with the ornament, and finally, the poem was meant for me. My entire being awaits his response. *Please don't be married...*

"Home is safety."

"Safety in numbers?" *Cut the desperate tone, Ava. You are a Wylder!*

"Numbers just make for a bigger target. I live alone on Nartan's land."

His empty bed shouldn't release butterflies in my belly. He's more nervous about the listening townspeople than displaying any attraction to me. Anyone passing by wouldn't believe we are conversing with each other. He is studying his shoes with his body facing the street. I wasn't kidding when I said I don't share, especially attention. I step forward so my toes touch his. Our rabbit fur boots match. The image of my smaller toes alternating with his larger ones shouldn't make me smile so widely.

His head snaps up. Large black pools stare at me with vulnerability. His cold shoulder is hiding a cauldron of desire, not indifference. I'm drunk with power. I could destroy this man or make him the happiest one on earth. Are his hands shaking or his whole body? The vibrations ripple indecently along the front of my dress, and my lace collar waves between us like scandalous fingers. Of all the suitors I met in New York, none of them stirred a reaction so strongly within me as Ikshu. What is it about him?

"Since I'm holding your horse hostage, I guess I

have detained you as well," I whisper the words along his chin. I breathe in the spicy scent of leather, tobacco, and cloves between each word I speak. I want anything I can get from him. He steps back, and I give chase.

"Tell me, Ikshu, are you the secret admirer who has dropped the furry boots and gloves on my doorstep? I just love them but haven't a clue who to thank."

He nods slowly and swallows. I love how he isn't as tall as my other suitors have been. A slight incline of his chin and we are eye to eye. Would he faint if I closed the distance and kissed him? Would the worn leather stretched across his chest feel warm from his skin? Standing between our horses, our chances of being seen are quite slim…

"I can't bear the thought of you being cold." The gravel quality of his voice conveys its disuse.

"And the ornament?"

"The stone is cordierite which gives its owner sweet dreams. I—"

"Dreams of you?"

"Not if it displeases you—"

"Because that what it has done. I dream of you and all the beautiful things you have shown me."

"Me?" The word is more squeaked than spoken.

"How about I release you if you show me something else beautiful? Take me somewhere, Ikshu. Let's disappear and exist somewhere beautiful, if only for a few moments. I need fuel for my sweet dreams tonight." With my heart on the line, I step out of his space. He could easily step around me to swing onto his horse and hightail it for the hills. The look on his face suggests he is considering doing just that. His eyes dart from the horse to me and back again. I hold my breath, so I don't

73

spook him more than I already have.

He nods with a smile rivaling the sun.

"Lead the way, please," I say before turning to Lady. Ikshu is there to lift my elbows as I mount my horse. The innocent contact warms patches where he had his hands on my sleeves and ignites a fireball in my system. The time it takes for him to mount his horse is not enough to recover my wits. My brain is scrambled.

Ikshu's horse, FoolsGold, tears out of town as if the horse and owner can't get out of Wylder fast enough. Lady is content to lope behind them, so I get a delicious view of Ikshu's assets. "Thank you, Lady. Riding slightly behind them is a fantastic idea," I whisper to the horse. She snorts in response.

Over the rolling prairie, we head northwest beyond the town limits and the common green. Ahead, the mountains loom over the wild landscape and blot out the sun. We travel into the shadows. I press Lady to ride closer to FoolsGold as we leave my stomping grounds. Finn's head would spin like a top if he knew how far I had strayed from Wylder with Ikshu as my only means of protection.

The image bubbles a giggle from my belly. The sound calls Ikshu's attention. I'm shocked to my toes when he chuckles in response. The rusty sound rolls over the planes like a summer breeze, out of place on this winter day. We laugh at nothing as we enter a place so private not even the sun can reach us. When Ikshu stops, I bring Lady to his side and begin to dismount.

"No, stay on her," he says with his hand on my elbow. The nerve endings in my arm come alive at his touch. If I were to topple out of my saddle, would he hold me in his arms? If he did, would I go up in flames? I busy myself adding my heavier gloves to Lady's pouch, so I have a moment to cool down.

"They are coming, and I want you to be able to outrun them if necessary."

"They?" Fear skitters down my spine. The shadows that were beautiful when we first arrived now add danger to the open grassland. Who would be meeting us in the middle of nowhere?

"Are you scared?"

"No," I snap. "Besides, I love being scared." When his eyebrows reach his hairline, I cower. "Being scared means I'm on an adventure. My life is dull, Ikshu. Thank you for showing me a secret place, but I —"

My words are cut off by the pounding of hooves. There must be a million beasts headed for us. Lady dances with nervous energy only to be sheltered by FoolsGold. The stallion rubs his head along her neck, and she quiets. As terrified as Ikshu was in town, I now mimic his body language. My head swivels as I strain my ears to hear. What monster moves so fast yet holds such weight? How far away are the beasts? Are they heading this way?

"Stay beside me, and I will protect you." Ikshu's promise rings of an oath meant for churches and ceremonies, not an afternoon ride. The chaos in my mind slows as I absorb his quiet serenity. He maneuvers FoolsGold to crowd Lady against a rocky outcropping. Before I can stop them, my hands grip his bare forearm. His heat, strength, and security bleed through my gloves.

The ground quakes, and the two trees in the distance sway at the edge of the mountain's shadow. The first bison rounds the corner and heads for the grassy patch between the two trees. Its mane swings with each step.

One by one, bison thunder past us to crowd in the last sunny spot. I have never been so close to one. My place is usually so far away they look like dots. However, each animal is larger than most of the buggies in town. A bison's head is taller than I am.

The last animal of the herd runs past us. The noise stops. They huddle together in a clump of brown fuzz, so all the members share the warmth of the small space. What was once a terrifying procession is now a benign backdrop. My heart pounds to the rhythm that had been set by the migration. I have a death grip on Ikshu's arm. I loosen the hold but refuse to let go completely. Oh, have I left a mark? Am I wicked for being pleased to have my fingerprints upon his person?

"I have never seen anything like it. They are bigger than I ever imagined." Why am I the breathless one when the bison did all the running? We sit in the stillness, and I shamelessly hold onto him. The silence is not awkward but peaceful. I absorb his energy, and it quiets the spinning thoughts that plague my mind. The constant ache in my head stops. The clutter clears, and I'm left with the majesty of nature…and the presence of the man beside me.

"What they represent is even bigger," he says in the direction of the herd.

"What do you mean?"

"This is one of the only herds out of a dozen left, and it is dwindling in size. Their migratory paths have been carved into homesteads with owners who do not allow them to cross. The government blames the tribes for hunting them, but we have coexisted for generations."

"So they are precious," I whisper. For several

minutes, there is no sound other than the odd bison grunt or horse complaint. The air stills. I experience a kaleidoscope of emotions from fear to awe to despair. My family built Wylder. Wylder, which seems so small, is huge when it cuts the migratory paths of the majestic bison. I search Ikshu's face for condemnation and find none. He either doesn't know I'm a Wylder or holds no ire toward the townspeople.

"At one point, the bison were more valuable than anything in my life. Times are changing though, and Nartan has told my family we are changing with them. I think the new path suits me. I'm tired of my future being dictated by a beast."

"How?"

"The Arapaho use hunts not only to provide for the tribal circles but as a rite of passage for young braves. My brother wears feathers, but I do not because he has proven his manhood while I haven't."

"Could have fooled me." The words fly out before I can censor them.

When he frowns at me, I add another shovel of coal to the fire. "When I cowered from the herd, I hid behind a man. You look like one. Smell like one. You feel like one too." I make a show of lowering my chin to the hands I have yet to remove from his arm. "Thank you for showing me something hardly anyone else will ever see in their lifetimes. I wasn't reading about someone else's special adventure. You gave me one of my own. I felt special today. You have an eye for beauty, and I want to follow you, so I get to see it too." My voice takes on a husky quality as I trace the symbols on his arm with my gloved finger.

His hand lifts, dislodging mine. My chin lifts to

protest when it is captured in his palm. I lean into him on instinct. He leans toward me so our foreheads touch. I close my eyes.

"With all the surrounding beauty you speak of, why can't I take my eyes off you?" he whispers over my lips. His voice is temptation luring my inhibitions from my head.

I connect our lips in a swift movement. I pour the emotions I have collected from his innocent touches into the kiss. The tentative sweep of his lips across my mouth awaken my primal side, and I take control. My hands frame his jaw, and his stubble catches on my gloves, holding them captive.

Decorum be damned, I lean as far as Lady will allow me. He catches me in his arms and presses my folded arms to his chest. I would climb into his skin if I could. I want the quiet beauty he brings to life. My goals are forever changed. I am no longer running from the noise of New York. I am running to the silence in Ikshu's arms.

Chapter 10

My lips have tingled for three days with no sign of relief. I may have signed my death warrant by kissing Ava Wylder, but at least I will die smiling. She nearly toppled us off our horses with her aggression like a she-bear defending her den. Susceptibility to female power must run in the family since that's what has made my brother act out-of-character…a she-bear.

I'm just as smitten with Ava, but it must stop before I have the whole town of Wylder demanding my head. I imagine a mob holding torches and pitchforks when guns would be more efficient. Just when I had found my way to integrate my business into town, I ruin it. How can I show my face there? I am terrified of the impending ambush by Ava's brothers.

All day I try to sew boots for beading when my brain focuses on them. Once Nartan returns from the reservation, I will have bags upon bags of decorations for them. I gave Nartan more money than ever to buy bits of bone, glass, and dyed teeth. Will they be shaped into beads, or will I have to do that? Good thing it is winter, and the tanning operation is frozen until the temperatures rise. I can show Olive how to shape beads. She is bored beyond belief in her cabin. She complains about it several times a day. It will please Nartan too if Olive is working on a project that doesn't involve killing anything.

"Ouch!" I howl when I jab myself with the porcupine quill for the hundredth time. Ava's stormy eyes float across my mind's eye. When we parted after the bison grazing, she didn't want to leave. I made up some phony excuse about Nartan having a curfew. Neither of us believed me. Her face was crestfallen, and I couldn't bear her feeling my rejection. Perhaps it is for the best though. Why does the thought lodge a rock in my chest? Is one kiss worth risking not only my business but my life?

What about the lives of Olive, Nartan, and the babies? If an angry mob storms the homestead, Nartan will defend it. Olive will too. I could destroy everything. I constrain my obsession with Ava Wylder to my dreams for the babies. They better be cute.

"Whoa there, Lady. We made it." Ava's voice carries over the homestead and into my teepee.

Outside, I verify my imagination has conjured her voice only to be knocked flat. Ava is tying Lady to the post in front of Olive and Nartan's fine cabin. Of course, she would assume I lived there. It is the only cabin on our property, and it is at the end of the road. She would be shocked to learn I live on the opposite side of the stream with the stinking tanning vats.

"Well, who might you be? I'm Olive Muegge. Welcome to the Sagebrush Homestead, darlin'."

Oh, no. Oh, no. Oh, no. I race to Ava, but Olive is only a few paces away and starved for company. If the two strike up a friendship, Ava will be here all the time. I can't continually reject her. I couldn't resist her before our kiss. Now my body is in overdrive. As I run to the cabin door, I lose certainty I will get rid of Ava. My tender heart wants to keep her.

"Hi, Olive. I'm Ava. I think we met at the Christmas party. I can't be certain as I met a dozen new people, and social events aren't my forte."

"You did mighty fine, Ava. We might have met, but Gotti was talking my ear off about his intended, such a sweet little thing. I never forget a face. What brings you all the way out here?"

I reach the women only to get starstruck by Ava. She is wearing a dark blue dress and matching hat with blue feathers reaching for the sky. The color brings out the tiny green flecks hidden in her storm-cloud eyes. Those flecks grew into vines after our kiss which snared my heart in her clutches. It isn't until her cheeks flush I realize I have been staring at her for a few minutes while the women watch me.

"Don't mind Ikshu. He is house-trained. He just isn't much of a talker." Olive means well but makes me feel like a beetle crushed under her boots.

"Actually, it is Ikshu I came to see. I love my new gloves so much I brought him a pie—"

"What kind of pie?" Olive's eyes go round with greed. As horrible as her cooking is, her appetite is legendary. Since my brother won't let her hunt at night in her condition, she has nearly eaten us out of house and home. She eyes the humungous confection in Ava's arms with an unabashed adoration I assumed she reserved for Nartan.

"It's a sweet potato pie with chestnut butter topping. It is to thank Ikshu. I don't have many talents and wanted to give him the most beautiful thing I could." She swings a shy smile at me and my heart drops to my toes. If she wants heart-stopping beauty, I should give her a mirror. Panic seizes my chest, and self-preservation kicks in.

"You shouldn't travel out here alone. In fact, you shouldn't travel here at all." I wish the words came out with the authority of my brother. Instead, they are released with the hesitation of a man about to do stupid. The result is more of a question than a statement, let alone a command.

"These roads are dangerous, especially with the sun setting so early. Ikshu will escort you back to town after we eat the pie," Olive says before licking her lips. To my horror, she loops her arm through Ava's and turns her toward the cabin.

"Wait, Olive, you don't—"

"Ikshu Sagebrush, if you think you are going to deny me a piece of pie and the company of Miss Ava, you are sorely mistaken. I will skin your hide and tan it if you turn this flower away. The nerve! Please excuse my squirrelly little brother. He would be a hermit if we let him."

"I would love to be a hermit too," Ava says with a coy smile. The "with you" hangs in the longing look she gives me before mounting the first step into the cabin. Like a bee lured by the scent of nectar, I follow the women into the cabin. If only Nartan were here to sort this out. Then again, I would have to tell him about the kiss. Never mind.

"Tell me more about the gloves, the pie, and yourself, Ava," Olive says before setting the kettle on the stove. A few months ago, she didn't know what a kettle was. Now she acts like a regular settler wife. I stand in the doorway with a gaping mouth. What will Ava say? I stalked her, bombarded her with gifts, lured her away from town, and assaulted her. *Oh, my lord.*

"Well, I fell in love with everyone's boots at the

Christmas party. Then I hear the scuttlebutt they are made by Ikshu and I wanted a pair. I love them and have only taken them off to sleep," Ava says with a feminine giggle. "I just had to have the matching gloves. Ikshu was kind enough to make them for me after we crossed paths at the common green, or was it at the gunsmith? My home is behind the shop, so I see all those who do business with Cyrus. I love the holsters Ikshu made in the window. I would buy them all, but I don't carry a gun to put in them. I'm tempted to buy them anyway and stuff them with pens."

The combination of half-truths and jumbled lies roll off her tongue with practiced ease. No twitches to her face or shifts to her eyes. She's a card shark wrapped in layers of lacy fabric. The tale she weaves draws me in. I plunk into the seat across from her at the large table at the center of the room. Olive hands Ava a knife before setting the pie and plates before her. Knowing how well she lies, I would hesitate in handing her a weapon. They would never find our pieces. The delicate creature who has invaded my life has more to her than meets the eye.

"Ikshu went into the gunsmithy?" Olive narrows suspicious eyes at us.

She falls right into Ava's trap or maybe it was intended for me because I have the opportunity to defend Ava's story with truth. "I did a drop-off a few days ago on my own. I promised Nartan I would manage the business until the babies come into the world. I met Cyrus at the Christmas party, so it was easy."

"Well, I never…" She stops with her hands on her hips and her giant belly pointing proudly at us. "Ikshu, by golly, you are growing up." My face generates more heat than the stove. Why does she have to make me sound like a kid in front of Ava?

"He is going up in the world," Ava replies with a slice of pie balanced on her knife. "I have been telling everyone about my boots who will listen. It would be a dream to work more closely with him."

My tongue rolls to the back of my mouth as I choke on her words. She said, "with him" not "with his art." How did I become entangled in her web so quickly? Has the time to preserve my life passed when I wasn't looking?

"You see," Ava says, setting a plate of pie in front of me, "my family owns Wylder Mercantile. We would love to sell boots in various sizes within our store."

"I…but…I…" I can't form words. Too many objections swirl in the tornado of panic brewing in my mind. Any one of them would suffice, but they are crowded at the gate between my mind and my mouth. Nothing can get through. Olive gives me the stink eye while bringing the coffee to the table. She sweetens to molasses when she sees Ava gave her a pie slice the size of Texas.

"Of course, silly me," Ava says with a palm to her forehead. "Your boots, jewelry, beading, ornaments, and anything else would be a perfect fit with the Wylder family. Anything you are offering, Ikshu, I want it." She locks eyes with me and leans on the table. In another life, at another time, I would have swept her into my arms and carried her off into the sunset. She wants what I offer but can't she see I have nothing to give? A lady like her won't last a minute sleeping in a teepee all night while tanning leather all day. She loves her books while I can't read. Her soft hands have never had to work like I would need her to every day.

"A business meeting was the last thing I expected when you rode up, Miss Ava. We would be delighted. I usually broker deals for Ikshu on account of his quiet nature," Olive says between shovels of the pie.

Ava looks to me for my opinion. The admiration woven with the green flecks touches a place deep inside my heart—a place I didn't know I had. I love the way she is looking at me as if I am the man of the house with the final say. In her eyes, I am a leader, a hero, a brave, and the man for her.

I spoon a piece of pie into my mouth before I say something stupid. I have a feeling any word would get twisted in Ava's master plan. Earthy root vegetable fills my mouth followed by the sweet sting of sugar. The meatiness of the chestnuts smooths the flavors to give the bite a savory finish. The filling dissolves in my mouth like a cloud. The crust flakes and crunches between my teeth, releasing sweet butter with each pass.

"Tell me you like it," Ava whispers. She holds her breath as if my opinion matters the world to her. Has anyone asked me my opinion, let alone waited for it like the colored leaves waiting to drop from the trees at the end of autumn?

"The best I've tasted," I whisper. Her shoulders droop from their protective position, and her spine straightens.

"Honey, if you bring 'round a pie like this when my husband is home, he will adopt you on the spot." Olive has eaten half her slice and is already eyeing a second. Ava is lucky Olive is so focused on the pie she missed the undertones of our conversation. Or was it by design? Was the pie a gift or a calculated diversion? What was once delicious turns to sand in my mouth.

The women laugh together while I sit and stew. Olive launches into tales from before she became a Sagebrush. Ava hangs on every word as Olive describes her life as a nomad. She asks Olive questions about what it is like to sleep in a teepee, to eat pemmican, and to listen to stories around a tribal circle's fire. Olive's account isn't tinted with nostalgia, but Ava latches onto the adventure while stepping over the hardships. What is she thinking?

"I thought I would be cooking for my family when I came home from school, but my brothers have moved out and my father is often out with his friends. Can I have permission to bring my creations out to you, Olive? We could be great friends."

"Of course, honey. We would be happy to keep you company. Where were you in school?"

"New York, but don't worry. I'm not going back." The jump in Ava's voice is the first sign of nervousness. Does she have commitments in New York? If so, she has no reason to hide from us. She must know we have no connections in the Old States.

"Well, you need to be getting back to town. The sun is setting, and I don't like Olive being here alone after dark."

Olive opens her mouth to protest and shuts it with a snap. She wants to assert herself as a shifter who has lived her life on her own terms. Shifter or not, she's carrying Nartan's world. Nartan would throw a tantrum if she let Ava in on her secret identity. So far, the people of Wylder are accepting of Arapaho men when tempered with her gentle presence. I doubt we could return the favor if they knew she could transform into a black bear.

The women hug and make silly promises of more

pie-filled visits. That's not happening. Funny how Olive uses her large belly to obscure Ava's view of the rest of the pie. Ava makes no move to reclaim it but instead links her arm around my elbow to be escorted out. She took off her gloves to eat so her bare palm rests on my forearm, which is also bare because I gave my cuff to her on the common green. Heat transfers between us until my insides coil like a rabbit ready to dash into the bushes.

"Shall we?" Ava asks innocently. I close the door to Olive's cabin behind us and lead Ava down the stairs to where Lady waits.

"I will retrieve FoolsGold from the barn, and we can be on our way." I yank back my arm, but Ava's grip has the strength of a snake squeezing its prey.

"Certainly, he will have to be brushed before being saddled. We will keep you company. If I remember correctly, he was quite fond of Lady." Ava steps into my space as she asks the question. I step backward and jab my thigh on the arm of the water pump.

"I can ride bareback," I say gruffly. I panic. This is going exactly how I want it and not want it at the same time. I would love to spend more time with her under the stars, but someone must be waiting for her at home. Someone who bought a shotgun from Cyrus. She has three men in town who are supposed to be looking out for her, and she has managed to give them all the slip. Soon her luck is going to run out, and I do not want to be a part of it.

"Oooh, you can? I have only read about men who ride without a saddle in my books," she croons. Those stormy eyes lock onto me, and I'm lost. She sees me as a stand-up fellow, and I'm not virtuous enough to correct her.

"Follow me," I say with my best impersonation of my brother's gruff tone. "I can at least tell you about the buildings on the homestead as we make our way to the barn."

She squeals with delight and claps her hands before untying Lady's reins. I step off the road to cross in the grass, but that is as far as I get. Ava's little hand is back on my arm as greedy as a hawk's talons. "So Olive's cabin only has two rooms. Where do you sleep? Do you have a cabin in the woods?" She bobs her head to look through the trees with anticipation.

"I sleep in the teepee, there," I say with a finger extended to my humble home. I hadn't noticed the faded painting or the way the skins were fraying at the bottom until now. A gray ring stains the top from repeated fire burnings without cleaning between them. "Nartan and I built it four years ago as the first building to claim this as Sagebrush land. Next, we redirected the Medicine Bow River to create the ankle-deep stream across our land and planted a garden on the hilltop. We built the first of the three small smokehouses next with matching brining vats to build a leather tanning business."

I guess I can blame the business for my lack of upkeep on my home. I'm too cowardly to gauge her expression. We walk in silence a few paces until I help her over the stream. One slender hand holds my arm hostage while the other snakes over my shoulder to caress my back briefly. With nowhere else decent to look, I chance a meeting of her eyes. They aren't filled with disgust but a familiar fire I've come to associate with her.

"Show me the inside, Ikshu."

"What? Why?"

"Because everyone's house looks the same in New York, but you live somewhere special. Being a guest in your room would be an adventure I would treasure." I hope Ava didn't mean the double meaning to her words, but the sly smile curling the bow of her lips tells me otherwise.

"It wouldn't be proper, Miss Ava. You came here as a lady when you showed up riding sidesaddle and wearing cotton gloves under the winter ones I made. I am not taking your dignity tonight." I pull her until she reluctantly walks with me to the barn.

"Being a lady is overrated. I am withering away with boredom, but every second I'm with you, I'm learning, growing, and experiencing. Ikshu, don't you see? You have the ability to give me life."

"That's being a bit of a flannel mouth, isn't it?" I ask the question while holding open the barn door for her.

"Prove me wrong."

"Some other time, perhaps. For now, I'm delivering you back to your home before your reputation is ruined." I mount FoolsGold to illustrate my point. Ava scowls at me before gathering her skirts between her legs. The little minx spread-knee mounts Lady like an outlaw.

"Then I will race you, Ikshu. Last one to Wylder House kisses the other one goodnight," Ava calls before rushing into the night.

"Ava, you are headed the wrong way," I call behind her. FoolsGold trots behind the mare on his own accord as if he's stepped up as her protector—whether I agree or not. He can easily overtake Ava's horse which makes her wager all the more ridiculous. *Wait*…I don't want to win and have to initiate a kiss, do I? *Snap*. The reins crack, and FoolsGold doesn't need any convincing to catch his girl. "Wylder is this way!"

Chapter 11

"You are going to get caught coming here every day. I don't like you on the road alone." For the fourth day in a row, I have come back from the common green with our flock plus a certain socialite from town. Each evening, I let her win our race back to town, so she kisses my cheek in the alley behind her home.

My soul is dangerously close to depending on Ava to be at my side. I dream of someday kissing her and not a chaste peck on her cheek. This morning, she didn't arrive until I was leaving, and I was distracted by her absence.

The squeezing noose around my heart unraveled when Lady appeared on the horizon. Ava's hair was unbound, so it trailed after them like golden rays of sunlight. They ran past us toward the homestead, and like his namesake, my stupid horse gave chase, forgetting the flock struggling to keep up.

"Then you should fetch me in the morning."

"Ava, you know I can't. People will talk, and when your family finds out—"

"I have it all under control. I slipped out from under my brother's nose this morning. Oh, don't look so shocked, Ikshu. Finn was going to visit eventually, so I mentally prepared for it." Ava leans back on the skin stacks she called a couch in my teepee. She may innocently think I use a bedroll on the stacked leather floor, but I have a suspicion she knows she is practically sprawled across my bed. Her pose is as casual as our conversation, but the heat in her eyes gives her desires away.

"Yet you are still here...did they accept our friendship?" My breath hitches. We lock gazes until her eyes fall to her lap. I guess she found a lie to use instead of telling them about me. "Ava, sometimes I wonder if I could be any man and you would share your time with me."

"Take it back," she says with blazing eyes. "I have been courted by half of New York. Worms with titles who wanted my money, walking pastries who needed constant praise, and haughty heirs who had never accomplished anything for themselves wanted my time. I couldn't wait to get away from them. I don't want a title, a manor, or a fortune from them. I want to see the beauty in the world with you. You are the only one on this planet who can make the hammers in my head stop pounding."

Tenderhearted, weak of body, and feminine in interests, who is she kidding in her pursuit of me? The taunts of the other boys from the tribal circle cloud my brain. I couldn't hunt, fight, or witness violence because I couldn't bear causing others pain. The prayers of the kill couldn't console me, and my mother took action.

I'm haunted by her sacrifice. She allowed the Shaman to remove four of her fingers as a gift to the Gods in exchange for unlocking the brave inside me. When it didn't work, I don't know who was more devastated—me or her. These memories threaten to unleash the tears I put away years ago.

Do I dare wish that Ava can see my true self and still

wants me? No one sees the man inside of me even though I don't think he is hidden. I reach inside my soul with a deep breath. Could Ava be my destined soulmate? I study her with new interest.

"I'm not ready to tell my brothers. I love having a secret place to escape and cannot bear it if they take this freedom away. My visits are deliciously scandalous, and I love having a story. My life has been so sheltered and boring. I just can't go back to simply existing. You understand…"

Her words scrape my heart until it is shredded to ribbons. Her freedom. Her story. Her scandal. Never once does she mention feelings for me or gratitude for my company. She's playing games when I am stupid enough to wish for more. I shut down the secret place in my heart that yearns for a soulmate. It's obviously not her.

"…and Finn was sitting at our kitchen table. Would you believe it? Ikshu…Ikshu? Are you listening to me?"

"Yeah, I fogged out. Sorry," I say sheepishly.

Ava gives me a half-smile before leaning to where I'm sitting on the floor. She puts her palm on my jaw and tilts my mouth toward her. "I forgive you," she whispers against my lips. A small peck and she's back upright as if it never happened.

"When Finn came over this morning, I had the bear signs cooling. He assumed I made them for a big family breakfast. That's why I was late to the green. I had to sneak the doughnuts into a sack between their visits to the stove!" Her eyes twinkle with mischief like a sprite who has made it snow in August.

"You shouldn't risk the trip without telling them. If something happened, they would be worried sick trying to find you. If your house burnt down, they would assume you were in it."

"If you are so worried about their feelings, why don't you throw me out?"

"Because I am a selfish man at my core. I treasure every minute I get to look at you and listen to your voice. You fill the silences in me, and I'm not ready to give you up." I let her see the truth in my eyes.

"Good, because you will never have to. I convinced them I am using the bear signs to bribe a seamstress at the dressmaker's shop to mend my dress." She pulls her navy-blue dress from a bundle Lady was carrying. The ruffle at the hem hangs from a few strings.

The sight lifts the corners of my mouth and frees a chuckle from my chest. The dress got caught on a burnt cottonwood tree when we tried to race after her first visit. Ava was yanked off her horse and into my arms, but the dress couldn't be saved. She looked at me with stars in her eyes and called me her hero. I carried her home in my lap at her insistence, but my fight was less than half-hearted.

"You are welcome to my spool box and porcupine quills. I keep them in the wooden chest in the corner. I think I have a blue to match, if not there is plenty of black thread."

"What?" Ava sputters and gasps like I just asked her to wrestle a bison.

"You didn't expect me to sew your dress, did you?"

"Well, yes, but—"

"I'm not doing it." I refuse only because she expects it. I never offered. Her frown pinches her brows together, and her lips into the shape of a heart. Childish expressions look adorable on her.

"Not even if I ask nicely?" she asks with a fake batting of her eyelashes.

"Especially if you ask nicely." I shake my head and give her a mean face copied from my brother. She can't hold her farce, and we laugh hysterically. She fetches the chest, and I help her root through its mess to find the tools to mend the dress. Soon we are sewing in silence, basking in the serenity our synergy brings.

"It's snowing," Ava squeals as I finish my third pair of men's boots. She abandons her half-mended dress to run outside barefooted. A blast of cold air enters the teepee as the canvas flap waves behind her. I slip on my boots and snag hers before joining her.

"You don't need your toes to enjoy it, but I'd rather you didn't lose them to frostbite." She freezes at my voice and chuckles on the journey back to the teepee. She takes a boot from my hand and uses the other to balance on my shoulder to put it on. The touch of her hand burns her print on my skin as if she tattooed it there. When she switches to the other foot, she stumbles with a fit of giggles.

Instinct takes over.

I grab her waist to steady her. With the boots in place, her arms are free to tangle around my neck. I crane my neck toward Olive's cabin only to be brought back to the front by Ava's gentle hand. It is the day of the full moon, so Olive is more likely in the forest than the cabin. Can she see, or is the teepee blocking the view? Do I dare?

"Why, Ikshu, this is forward," she says in her fake flirty tone. I love it when she uses this voice to make fun of the society woman she is supposed to be. It lulls my heart into the safety of her willingness to rough it here with me. "Have you asked for my hand or simply decided to bypass them for my waist? I have to admit I find the latter much more to my liking."

I retract my hands as if she's on fire. She doubles over with laughter. She slaps her knees and holds her middle as she fights for air. I am compelled to join in just because she is so ridiculous and outrageous.

Half the time, she's stalking me like a wolf, and the other half she's pushing me away. Maybe she was put in my path as a lesson. I need to lighten up. Her inner sunshine brightens my world, which is a huge burden for her to carry alone. I need to take some of the load and stop being a stick in the mud.

I grab her waist once more and swing her around in a circle. Her squeals of delight are music to my ears. A menacing growl from the forest cuts our laughter short. Ava shrieks and tries to climb me like a tree. I recognize the curly-haired black bear as my sister-in-law. The wild mane and hanging pregnant belly are a dead giveaway.

"Let me show you the most beautiful thing in the world," I whisper to a terrified Ava. As much as I love her pressed against me, her fear rakes at my insides. She trembles in my arms but nods when she sees I'm smiling.

"I trust you, Ikshu."

I shift her behind me but allow her to stay coiled around my arm. I stoop to make myself less threatening and advance slowly to the bear. Olive roars and shakes her head. She doesn't agree with what I'm about to do, but I am drunk on the power of impressing Ava. "It's okay…She's safe…I promise…I wouldn't do anything to endanger you," I whisper to Olive.

"Her roaring tells me she doesn't believe you. Shouldn't we be trying to get away from the bear before she eats us," Ava whispers against my ear. Tendrils of her hair tickle my jaw interlocking with the stubble there. I wish to show her I'm as special as she thinks.

"Come on, little sister. Do you think I would risk Nartan's wrath to endanger you?"

Olive whines and paws the ground before trundling to my feet. I kneel slowly while dragging Ava to crouch on the ground. Ava's panicked breathing presses her bosom against my arm with each pant. A better man would soothe her by revealing Olive's identity. As if I'm the master of the forest, I rub the fur between Olive's ears. She prostrates at my feet. Ava gasps behind me. I pull her by the wrist to my side and place her hand on Olive's head. Olive growls at Ava's touch but doesn't move to strike her.

"See, Ikshu, there's no other man on the planet who could give me this moment." Ava's whisper makes me feel ten feet tall. Now who is playing games instead of living in reality?

Chapter 12

Heave, Ho! Heave, Ho! Sweat flows down my spine as I chip away at the frozen ground. I started with a shovel but quickly changed to a pickax to burrow into the January-hardened dirt. *Phew!* The hole I have made is not big enough for a grave, let alone a foundation for a cabin to rival Nartan and Olive's.

A cabin was the beginning of their romance, and look how it turned out. Nartan's sun rises and sets with her smile. Surprisingly, she is equally as smitten with my moody brother. A year and a half ago, on a sunny day in June, my brother started digging a hole for a cabin. He hadn't met Olive but felt her spirit in the wind, or at least that's how he described it to me.

Ava's eyes shined with adoration akin to worship when I beckoned Olive's she-bear to us. Telling her Ephraim-shifter secret is the most selfish thing I could do, so I allowed Ava to believe I am a mystic bear whisperer. If we ever meet a real bear, we could be mauled to pieces. It would serve me right for acting so foolish. If Nartan were here, he would tan my hide in my own braining fluid. I haven't had the courage to face Olive since the incident. The right thing to do is to come clean to Ava with Nartan and Olive's permission.

However, step one is to ask Ava to join our little tribal circle. As my wife, she would be under Nartan's protection as our elected leader and entitled to knowing the magical secrets of my family. No city girl would accept the proposal of a man in a teepee, so I must build her a cabin. Our cabin will have two bedrooms though. She will need a quiet place to sleep when my nightmares claim me.

"Ikshu, what in tarnation are you doing?" I nearly jump out of my skin at my brother's outburst. His condescending voice manifests from my musings. When will I ever learn that what you think produces what you see? He must have returned last night and already had his reunion with Olive to have time to torment me.

"Building a cabin. It is time I have a cabin of my own."

"Soooo you are digging a foundation…"

"Yes"

"…in frozen ground…in the dead of winter…"

"It would go faster in the spring, but I would like to have it built by then."

"Oh, Ikshu," my brother sighs. He presses his fingers into his eyes to unsee my project. "I have neglected to give you guidance since Olive's arrival to our family. I'm sorry."

"I am finding my path, Nartan. I am the same age you were when we built the Sagebrush Homestead from the ground up. It is my turn build to a livelihood…and a family."

"I know you are looking for ways to grow up, and I'm sorry about the feathers, the rings, our fights, and all of it. How about I help you this spring the way you helped me? We will build the cabin of your ladylove's dreams. Together as brothers."

"She will be gone by spring."

"Wait, who? Did you meet someone in town? Olive

told me about your holster drop-off, and I came out here to praise you for it. Does Cyrus have a sister?"

"No, if you must know, I met Ava at the Christmas party." I choke on my words. Olive told him about my drop-off but not meeting Ava for pie or my using her she-bear to be impressive. I owe her an apology, gratitude, and another pie.

"Ava…I don't remember meeting an Ava."

"She was hiding behind the tree—"

"—like you were—" Nartan's softened features harden to their natural glare.

"Yeah, we fit because we are quiet. I can be myself around her."

"Well, I'm happy for you. The elders at the reservation helped me see I have been too hard on you. Their spirits told me that you will need my help more than ever in the coming days. While Olive's danger is far off, yours is immediate. We made this for you in the sacred circle."

Nartan reaches into his tobacco pouch and hands me a small calumet carved from bone. The pipe is a totem shape with a bear, an owl, and a buck imprinted on it. The bear is obviously Olive. I guess the know-it-all owl is Nartan. This makes me the buck. I smile at its full head of antlers. It has the twelve points of a full-grown male.

"I brought mine out here too." Nartan claps my shoulder and squeezes with affection. "Let me show you how to make a sacred space and see if my guides will call your teacher."

Nartan's pipe is packed with herbs, but mine is empty. He gives me a wad from his supply and shows me how to pack it into the pipe. He lights both pipes, and we smoke in silence. As the rancid smell of the mystery herbs fills the air, I try not to think about what is flowing into my body. I trust my brother not to poison me, but the smell is worse than our urine vats in the August heat. Every few puffs, Nartan looks at me with squinted eyes.

"What?"

"Why aren't you coughing and gagging like a normal first-timer?"

"I have to admit. I have used your pipe on a few quests to call in my spirit team with no success."

Nartan sighs and hangs his head. "Your guides will only come with your offering after your teacher invites them. My guides probably saw you and laughed. They always tease me and probably saw you as easy prey for their mischief. Did you open sacred space first?"

"I repeated your incantation, if that's what you mean."

"It is more than a group of words, Ikshu. Let's try it together." Nartan sits cross-legged on the ground, and I follow. "You need to bind yourself to Mother Earth first. Feel her loving energy grab your roots and flow up your body stopping at each spiritual center within you."

Nartan closes his eyes and lets his mouth hang open. I mimic his posture out of awkwardness rather than to learn it. My brother can be so strange. We sit for a moment in comfortable silence.

Then it hits me.

The energy sits below my belly button and builds to a swirling mass of heat. The heat reaches upward before wrapping around my ribs. A warmth spreads through my chest to fill the cracks in my heart. It flows into my throat to loosen the threads that have bound it closed for years. My forehead stings as the energy opens my third eye to the spirit plane. Finally, a crown of heat is placed on my head. The strangest sensation of the top of my head lifting off snaps my eyes open.

"Spirits who are enlightened may stay; spirits who are not enlightened must go for I am creating a sacred space in the name of Ikshu Sagebrush." My brother's voice booms across our land like a dust devil. My body feels lighter. Could he have chased away the demons from my nightmares?

Did he have the power to do so all along yet let me suffer each night? I don't dare ask and break the spell, not when he is sharing his mystical knowledge with me.

The wind picks up, and snow is pitched over us. I shake my head and bat at the onslaught, but my brother sits like a wooden statue. The ambush of flakes condenses into six man-like shapes. They are dressed in ceremonial outfits and stomp around us in a dance I have seen Nartan do a thousand times. When I make eye contact with one, he winks, and the hair on the back of my neck stands on end.

"Spirits of my ancestors, the Six Water-Pouring Men of the Sagebrush legacy, I introduce my brother, Ikshu Sagebrush." At my brother's command, the group stops to stare at me. They dissect me with their gaze like a carcass being divided into steaks.

"Pleasure to meet you," I whisper, not knowing what I'm supposed to do.

"Pleasure? Give them a few minutes," Nartan retorts under his breath.

"Phew, boy, how is it our legacy gets sourer with age?" The first Water-Pouring spirit asks the group.

"I wonder if we were brewing 'em instead of raising them. The funk these brothers are in rivals the strongest beer," another spirit quips. The group laughs and slaps each other on the back at our expense.

I look to Nartan for an explanation, and he rolls his eyes. "I have brought Ikshu to you to ask for his teacher."

"What this boy needs is his teacher," says one to the other. The group nods in agreement.

"That's what Nartan said." I can't help but stick up for my brother. His representation means the world to me. How can his guides laugh and joke at our expense?

"Ikshu, let them go. They are a squirrelly bunch. I can only hope you get more helpful, straightforward group of guides." At Nartan's words, the guides break out into laughter. They carry on while Nartan fumes. Perhaps Nartan's soul lesson is in humility because his guides are serving slices of humble pie left and right.

"Ohhhh, look who is almighty now!"

"A few months being the man of the house will do that to a fella." The ghosts continue their stomping but weave a small circular path around Nartan.

"Man of the house? More like coyote of the den. Look at the mangy mug he's wearing."

"He's just wearing a pucker because his face got stuck that way. Too much smooching if you ask me."

"Are you finished yet?" Nartan's temper hits the bursting point, and he detonates like a Fourth of July firecracker. "I called you to help my brother." Steam billows from his nose like a bull, which gives him a frightening appearance. The ghosts are hardly phased by my scary brother's show of force.

"Son, put the horns away. We aren't wearing red, so you aren't going to charge us anyway. Of course, we will call his teacher. Ikshu has been more patient than you were at his age," says the first spirit in a calm, fatherly voice.

The spirits dissipate into whirling snow, but this time I have the sense to duck. Nartan sits still with pride and gets rewarded with stinging lashes. The sensation of my spirit flying toward the heavens starts within me. I soar past clouds in my mind's eye at a dizzying speed. Four, five, on the sixth vapor level, Nartan and I are deposited on a pillow of clouds. My brother's cheeks and forehead are red with frost when the spirits condense once more.

A seventh spirit is with them. My teacher is a withered old man who carries a mask almost his size. He barely reaches the shoulders of Nartan's team and my heart sinks. Not only am I judged as weak in body and weak in mind, but I'm also weak in spirit guide. My teacher uses the mask as a cane as he hobbles toward me.

"Son, I don't need bodily strength because my body is not corporeal. I am frail in image only. Your strength in character is enough for both of us. What you need is wisdom, and I have it. It is not my power you should measure but the combined power we share."

"Your kind words humble me, great teacher. I am honored to be your student," I say with a tilt of my head in respect.

"See, Nartan, that's how you interact with your guides. Where's your humble bow, huh?" Nartan's guides start ripping into him again as soon as my words hit the air. My brother's windburned face turns purple as he holds his temper.

"I'm glad to have connected with you, Ikshu. You will need me more than ever in the next few days. You will have the greatest test of your life, and I want to be by your side for support."

"What do you mean he will be tested? What is the

nature of the test? How can I help?" Nartan's panic fires questions from his mouth like a quiver of arrows shot all at once. He not only hits his target but everything in a one-mile radius.

"Nartan, this is Ikshu's fight, because at the heart of the matter is a choice unique to him. He must stand on his legs, or she will not be his."

"She? She who? The only she in his life is Olive. What is going to happen to Olive? Is it the babies?" Nartan launches another round of questions at the speed of a hawk after a kill.

"Nartan—shut up," scolds his guide with the largest head roach. My brother's jaw drops and shuts. He's in full codfish mode at their asserting authority in front of me.

"Ikshu, she's going to bring a barnful of trouble down on your head. You know who I'm talking about."

"What if I want the trouble she brings?" My quiet admission shocks both my living and dead family members.

"Then call on me to help at any step of the way. I will see you through this Brave Ikshu Sagebrush of the Sagebrush Legacy." With the final ruling of my fate, we are dropped from the cloud as gentle as an early snowfall. When we reach earth, all seven spirits dissolve. Nartan gets hit in the face with snow again. This time, I have my wits gathered so I can join in the laughter at his expense.

Chapter 13

"See those clouds. Those are a snowstorm waiting to happen. I cannot let you come back to our homestead today. You will get stuck there. See, I have tobacco pouches instead of sheep. I'm heading into town and, thereby, walking you home." Ikshu looks so stern. How many times did he practice his speech this morning to deliver it in such a gruff tone?

"Well then, lead the way." He raises an eyebrow at my smirk but lets it go. We guide our horses at a leisurely trot, but my companion is anything but relaxed. He opens his mouth to say something, only to make eye contact with me and stop himself. The third time I giggle at him to make his cheeks flame red.

"Out with it, Ikshu."

"I have a confession."

"You are hopelessly in love with me?" The joke flies out of my mouth and lands on the ground with a squish. Why am I so insensitive? There is nothing he can say to save face. I grope for the words to apologize and come up with blanks.

"It's about the bear—"

"That was a huckleberry above a persimmon! I still can't believe how brave you were." I beam my brightest smile, and Ikshu shifts uncomfortably.

"No, I wasn't brave. I knew…you see the bear…" His words drift into whispers before his silence engulfs us.

"You knew the bear before yesterday? Are you downplaying your bear-whisperer abilities because you knew the bear wouldn't hurt us? Let me guess. You had interacted with that particular bear before and lived. Therefore, you had no fear for me, and now you are feeling guilty."

"You are close to the truth, but there's more—"

"I don't need the rest of the story then. Whether you tamed a bear yesterday or a year ago doesn't matter. Ikshu, you amaze me." This time, my smile is met with a matching expression. Of all the dumb things to be nervous about, Ikshu is too modest for his own good. His humility only adds to his charm in my book. He's the complete opposite of the blowhards who are supposed to be my match.

We fall into our usual comfortable silence with stolen glances and shy smiles along our secret route back to town. I relish the ride by the Medicine Bow River, over the plains to cross the railroad tracks far from the station, and around the common green instead of the direct road. The drab brown landscape is alive when I am beside Ikshu. It is as if his energy brings nature into focus. Without inane conversations about stupid topics like the weather or gossip, my mind is free to make animal shapes out of clouds and to discern the different herbal smells of the prairie. I just wish we didn't have to part behind the Calvary Office, so no one sees us together in town. *But oh*, the kisses we share when we reunite in the alley behind the Wylder House are deliciously scandalous.

"What has crinkled your brow?" His voice rumbles over my arms, and I shiver in delight.

"I was wondering if that cloud is rabbit-shaped or dragon-shaped?" I point to a blob to our left.

His face brightens. "I thought it was another one of your pies."

"You aren't getting another pie until I get a pie tin back. I think Olive has all three of them. I can't bake without a tin." My scolding loses its fire because it is broken with giggles. If a pie is what keeps Ikshu's pregnant keeper busy, so I get time alone with him, I will bake one in a wash bin. I'd bake all night just to spend all day at his side. When Olive mentioned Nartan's love of bear signs would point to adopting me, I imagined myself making heaps of doughnuts larger than bison.

"After the snowstorm, I can bring the pie tins to you. The snow will be too deep for you to travel, but I'm used to it." His offer is unexpected. On one hand, I would love to see him if only for a little while. On the other hand, I'm not anxious for him to meet my brother...or *good lord*, my father. When I hesitate, Ikshu purses his lips and looks at his lap.

"Never mind, you probably don't want me risking my safety either." He says to give me an out. Now I'm as lowly as a road apple. We both know the real reason is the scrutiny of Wylder society but refuse to admit it. We are silent as we cross town on Old Cheyenne Road. People stop and stare. Women pull their hats together to whisper.

If my brothers didn't suspect I was sneaking off before, the townspeople will give them ample cannon-fodder now. Funny, I can't seem to get worked up about it. Glancing at Ikshu under my lashes, I can't tell if he's bothered by the gossip. Our combined energy has wrapped around us in a loving cocoon where nothing matters but us.

We arrive at the corrals too quickly. He turns with a tip of his hat while I dismount from Lady. "Hurry home and tuck in before these clouds release their snow, Miss Ava. You aren't dressed for the coming weather."

"What can I say to make you stay?"

"Stay where, Ava?" He's right. If my house is off limits and his place is far away, where would we go? Where do we belong if we are together? The weight of our differences sits on my chest like a bucket of coal. For the first time in my life, I have no pithy comeback, know-it-all answer, or snappy retort. All I have is the sadness found somewhere between the life I want and the life I am supposed to live.

"Take care of yourself," he whispers and turns back to the tobacco shop. Tears well in my eyes, and my lips tremble. All the gawkers just watched Ava Wylder get brushed off by Ikshu Sagebrush, and I won't have it. They see a lowly Native. I see the one man who quiets my headaches. With his shy smiles, beautiful talents, and chiseled physique, I won't find a better man for me anywhere else. He's the blend of wild and responsible I need…if only I could convince him, he's the one.

I brush Lady with one eye to the 5-Star Saloon. The tobacco shop is behind it so Ikshu needs to cross the saloon doors before he turns toward home. If he stops for a drink, I'll know…he better not stop in for a drink…there could be dancing girls in there. The thought of Ikshu around dancing girls tightens my fists over Lady's brush. He's not into social scenes. He's Ikshu. I breathe away the tension and question the origin of my anger. It's not like he's my huckleberry.

He turns the corner, and his hat is tucked under his

arm. The soft black waves of his hair tumble to his elbows. I am too far to hear them, but I bet his shells are clinking with each step. He holds the reins on his hip to camouflage the way he drives the horse with his legs. Only a man used to riding bareback would have this talent. Too bad riding without a saddle is too improper for Wylder these days. Oh, how the way FoolsGold shifts Ikshu from side to side makes me wish to be very improper indeed.

A ray of sunshine peeks through Ikshu's ominous clouds and lands on Lady's back. Perhaps Ikshu the Wise isn't as clairvoyant as he thinks. I bet the snow doesn't come to town for hours. Even so, I could ride back when it starts. He's an hour away, not in the Old States. He will never let me join him, but he has no say in whether I follow him.

****

What has gotten into FoolsGold? He wants to go back to town so badly, he nearly grassed me twice. If it weren't for the upswing in the weather, I would let him lead. As it stands, I'm not going to explain to Nartan how I got stranded in the woods during a snowstorm while following a horse's intuition. No wonder my horse has "fool" in his name.

After fighting for control for an hour, I lead him into our barn. FoolsGold lets out his loudest complaint. "What is it, buddy? You are home now. Look, there's Strawberry, all settled and happy. Let's get this saddle off of you."

"Do you always offer comfort in the form of undressing?"

Eek! I shriek at the feminine voice echoing in our barn. Ava and Lady walk into the barn as if they own the place. Strawberry neighs at the newcomers while FoolsGold grins his toothy smile. Hand over my heart, I catch my breath. "Curses, Ava. You scared me to death. What are you doing out here? Didn't I warn you about the snow?"

"Oh Ikshu, you worry too much. When the flakes begin to fall, I'll go—"

"You can't return alone, and I will be stuck in town."

"Ikshu, there will be no bandits waiting on the road to ambush me during a snowstorm. Come on," Ava says in her no-nonsense tone. She ties Lady into the same stall as FoolsGold even though there is an open stall where we lamb young in the spring.

"Why are they so close?"

"Lady is used to having other horses close where she boards at the livery. Besides, they look smitten together." As if on cue, treacherous FoolsGold rubs his muzzle along Lady's neck. As much as Nartan has tried to mate him with Strawberry, he has never seemed interested. I guess he was holding out for Lady.

"Well, now that I am here, what can we do?"

"Take you home—"

"Don't be such a stick in the mud, Ikshu. Let's relax and wait for the snow to fall at least."

The growl of my stomach protests before I can. The rumble echoes through the barn. I wish I could melt into the floor. I stare at the boards as if I have a choice between which ones I get to slide.

"If only I had access to Olive's stove, I would cook us a lovely meal. You know I can cook as well as I bake. Perhaps I can use my skills as a bargaining chip if we are caught by Nartan or Olive," she says with a giggle. If only she didn't add sunshine to my life, I could resist her. Even the few rays of low winter sun have found a way to spotlight her. The light reflects from the golden strands woven into a knot at the back of her head, so she appears to glow. What would she look like with it flowing over the skins on my bed? Would it be as soft as it looks tangled around my fingers?

"I'll grab some pemmican under the guise of working alone for the night. They won't bother us in my teepee if they think I'm busy. Besides, I don't wish to subject you to anything else Olive makes." Just like that, I'm ensnared in Ava's web. I hear myself go from observer to co-conspirator in an out-of-body experience. What has possessed me?

Chapter 14

"I am always amazed at how fast time flies with you, Ikshu. Look, the light coming through the top of your teepee has dimmed. It is sunset already." I stretch my arms over my head. I have been hunched over my copy of "*Around the World in Eighty Days*" since choking down the pemmican he smuggled from Olive and Nartan. I didn't know pemmican was small animal jerky pounded with herbs and spices and dried. I may have been less enthusiastic about tasting it had I known.

His teepee is smaller than the formal sitting room in the Wylder house, but it is sheltered and cozy. It smells of herbs, leather, the wilderness, and best of all, masculinity. The best part is you could hear a pin drop, it is so quiet. The canvas blocks the sounds of the prairie, giving the place a timeless quality. It's like I achieved my goal of crawling into his skin for safekeeping.

"You need to leave. It is past time we tried to get back."

"Pony up? If I didn't know better, I would suspect you were giving me the mitten. Is she dark-haired or another blonde like me?"

"Ava, you are not being fair. I'm trying to keep us safe—"

I cut off his words by opening the door flap with a humph. A cold blast of snow slams into my face. My skin stings with the bites of flying ice pellets. My breath leaves my chest in a whoosh, and I'm doubled over in the fight to breathe. Ikshu scrambles to my side to close the flap, but it waves like a white flag of surrender in the wind.

"It's snowing sideways," I yell over the howling of the storm. Ikshu takes my shoulders and pushes me onto his couch. He uses his body to fill the doorway while scooping firewood from the side of the entrance into the teepee. His hair flies about his head. The shadow he casts is the shape of a raven, a foreboding shape on the floor. He traces the top of the doorway to gain purchase on the leather. His deft fingers tie knots in leather cording to hold it in place. The door is closed in seconds.

The security of silence returns.

His brow furrows with concern as he looks me over. I try to smile at him, but my teeth are chattering.

"You aren't even dressed for winter. How could I let my desire to be in your company overshadow your safety? It is too late to travel back to Wylder now." He wipes his hands down his face in frustration.

"I don't want to get back. I only want warmth." I pat the bed beside me and raise my eyebrows at him.

"We cannot build a fire until the wood dries. I…uh…had made this for you…to give you later but you aren't dressed for winter." He digs through the stack of buckskins, vests, and furry items. His leather pants scrunch and stretch over his backside with every movement. I'm still staring when he straightens with clothes draped over his arms. "They aren't decorated but the leather leggings will keep you much warmer than your…your…" He waves his hand over his knees in an adorable gesture.

"Thank you. I have wanted leggings connected to

slippers since I saw Olive's pair. You are right they will be much less drafty than my dress and bloomers." He turns red at the mention of my undergarments like I knew he would. I stand to examine the clothes closer.

The tunic may not be adorned, but it is stunning, nonetheless. Several pieces of leather are cut into rows of semicircles, giving the top half the appearance of layered feathers. The sleeves and bottom are cut and gathered into tassels just below a band of intricately carved birds. The same birds are carved where the legging meets the shoes.

"We can design their beading together or I can paint them if you like. I'll step outside so you can change into them."

"Don't you dare fight the weather again. Besides, who will open these buttons for me?" I turn my back to him and present the line of buttons trailing from collar to tailbone. Did he swallow his tongue with his loud gulp?

Of course, I fastened myself this morning and can unclasp my own dress. Only the top five need to be undone so I can pull it over my head. The rest is a decoration, but he doesn't need to know it. He steps close and starts with the top button. The backs of his fingers caress my neck and I shiver.

"Miss Ava, you are playing with fire," he whispers. His breath trails over the back of my neck. My eyelashes flutter in rapture as the teasing of his fingers moves lower. Goosebumps form over my arms when the cool air reaches for my exposed camisole. His fingers travel lower in hesitant strokes. I've watched his nimble fingers sew all afternoon, and my buttons aren't complicated. The knowledge he is savoring undressing me feels deliciously wicked. At the last button, he rests his hands on my hips.

I hold my breath.

He steps away and takes his heat with him. "You are free," he says. Never a truer statement was uttered. If I pressed the issue, I could be considered ruined for any other man. No more sissy suitors for me. Only a less-than-forced marriage to Ikshu would be proper then. The thought shouldn't fill me with bubbles of happiness.

"Thank you," I say in a breathy voice I hardly recognize. "If you hand me the tunic, I will put it over my head and then pull my dress out the bottom. You won't see anything I don't wish for you to see."

"That's exactly what I'm afraid of," he says with a sigh. The sheepskin tunic brushes my hair before I bring it over my head. It is much too large and hangs below my knees to an almost modest length. Olive's is as indecently short as I had wanted mine to be. I giggle when the sleeves hang over my hands.

"I must have misjudged how narrow your shoulders are in comparison to Olive's frame. I used her measurements for this." The frown in his voice is adorable. I shimmy out of my dress, and it pools onto the floor. Next on the pile are my petticoats. His retreat to the far reaches of the teepee makes a shuffling sound. I cannot hold my laughter at his delicate sensibilities. Just to rile him further, I remove my bloomers too.

"Then why is her tunic short and mine is long?" I ask over my shoulder. My arm extends to ask for the leggings while I step out of my settler clothes.

"Her baby belly stretched it," he says with shrug. He hands me the leggings and turns to face the canvas. I shake my head with a laugh. Legs apart, hands clasped behind his back, and chin raised, his posture suggests I'm holding him prisoner. "I tried to confess to you earlier, but I chickened out. There's something you must know about Olive and Nartan—"

"Are they your parents?"

"No, no, why does everyone think that? Olive and I are less than a year apart. Do I really look young enough?"

"Perhaps it is wishful thinking since I am barely over twenty. Your gentle nature implies youth, but your face is lined with age and your eyes haunted with experience." Dressed in sturdy leather, I no longer sense the drafts sneaking inside the bottom of the teepee. With each word, I boldly step toward him. When he turns to face me, I cup his chin in my palm. I raise to my tiptoes to kiss him, and he steps away.

"I need to tell you before we go any further. There is still a chance I deliver you to Nartan and we can save your reputation." He combs his fingers through his hair and paces with agitation. Nervous energy fills the small space, and the walls seem to close in. His panic fuels his quickening steps.

"Breathe, Ikshu." My words freeze his movements like a blast from the storm outside.

"Ava…Ava…my family has secrets. Secrets I want to tell you. I'm torn between keeping their secrets and bringing you into the fold. I cannot just tell anyone. I—I—"

"How about you look at it this way? If you tell me to 'bring me into the fold,' then I'm ready to hear them now. If you plan to reject me, my brother's will ship me back to New York on the next train, whether I'm keen to go or not. Either way, your secrets will be safe."

He stares with conflicted emotions.

"I'm completely harmless. Do you have a bowl or cup I can use to hold my hairpins?"

He hands me a small metal cup, so my pins clink the bottom as I release each golden curl. He's barely breathing as he watches me. Who knew such a mundane task could be so erotic? I slow my movements and thread my fingers through the locks as they are released, only because his eyes follow my every move.

"Ikshu, you will feel better to confess, and I won't judge you. Keep me or banish me, it doesn't matter what I know."

"I'm not a bear whisperer. I knew the bear was Olive trying to stop me from being too familiar with you. She is Nartan's soulmate because she's an Ephraim shifter. You see, he's a mystic who straddles our plane and the realm of spirits." His face is torn to pieces as if confessing to shooting my horse.

"You said the last thing I expected you to say," I say with a chuckle.

"Well, is that your reaction?"

"Ikshu, you are a storybook character come to life. Your every confession makes me more interested in you. I don't think a lifetime is enough to learn all the facets of you. I'm captivated…and a little embarrassed my life has been so boring in comparison."

"Ava, I have thought of hundreds of words to describe you, but boring has never been one of them. You are beautiful, smart, worldly, educated—" His words warm my heart until the flames are doused by self-doubt. If everyone in his life is gifted, it stands to reason he is too.

"What's your secret ability?"

"I'm just me. The elders didn't think I would grow

to be a brave, let alone a medicine man. I doubt I will ever develop magical powers."

"Fantastic." I clap my hands and jump up and down.

"Why?" He stands with his hands on his hips and his chin lifted to the side. He peers at me through squinted slits.

"Then you don't have a magical soulmate in the forest who will come to eat me!" I jump around with clapping hands to the music of his laughter. "Now that I'm officially safe. How can I entertain you?"

"WHAT!"

"I thought I could read to you. I've been reading to myself all afternoon when I could have been sharing the story of Phineas Fogg with you. Come and cuddle with me. I promise I won't shift into a bear and bite you." I climb under the mountain of furs on his bed and gesture for him to join me. His face mirrors a rabbit who has met a predator.

After a moment's hesitation, he steps close enough for me to grab his wrist. I pull him into bed and wait for him to get settled before covering us with the blankets. I lift his arm so I can nestle beneath it and wrap my leg around his. "Perfect," I sigh.

"This will get us skinned and tanned."

"Who cares? We would make a handsome pair of boots."

****

The low din of conversation outside of the teepee stops. I set down the brush I was tufting with porcupine quills. Grandmother Winter drops the tunic she was beading for my initiation into the Star Lodge. The pounding hooves should have brought the arrival of the hunting party, but no one is cheering. There was nothing.

119

It was as if the women and children of the circle were holding their breath.

Then the screams start.

Did the fire at our teepee center try to fly? Flames lick the top of the teepee reaching for the fire lit at our feet. The temperature soars and sweat beads on my arms. "Come, Grandmother, we must leave. Something about this fire scares me. Please let's go," I cry. I pull her arms with all my might to bring her to stand. I am a foot taller than her, but she is round from mothering and having a comfortable life. As I straighten, I smell the putrid stench of burnt hair before the searing pain registers.

I scream.

"No, no, no, Ikshu," Grandmother whispers. "You mustn't speak. You must not let them find us. Promise me you will be silent as we crawl out of the back of the teepee. Promise!" Her eyes are hollow, and her mouth is set into a grim line. Her color pales to ghostly.

A white hand attached to an inhumanly long white arm snakes into the teepee behind her. "No, Grandmother. Watch—" My words are cut off when the hand snakes around my throat. It threatens to squeeze the life out of me as it drags me out the door.

AAAH! I'm awake in my own bed, but I'm not alone. A white hand rests on my collar, dangerously close to my throat. It glows in the moonlight like the hand from my nightmare. *Ava.* I must have fallen asleep beside Ava Wylder. Was she always so pale? I'm caked in a cold sweat but boiling beneath the skins and her scalding limbs. Panic seizes my chest and I fight for air. I've got to get away from her. *Now.*

Chapter 15

"Spirits who are enlightened may stay. Spirits who are not enlightened must go, for I am creating a sacred space." Perhaps it is my chattering teeth, but the incantation always sounds more powerful when Nartan yells it. *Sigh. Cough, cough, cough.* Whose stupid idea was it to light a calumet in a smokehouse? *Oh yes, mine.* Imagine that. The three-foot square space fills with smoke. "Teacher, please help me."

Smoke rising to the ceiling reverses its course. It condenses into the figure in the opposite corner of the small chamber. Had my spirit teacher been as tall as Nartan, he would have bumped his head on the rod for hanging skins suspended from that corner. The little man is much shorter than I with his hunchback posture. He has lost some of his ghostly texture, so I can see the lines in his leathery skin. A tunic hangs from his bony frame as if it were his last remnant of a once muscular body. He leans on his cane with both hands folded, and I wait for my punishment. I asked for trouble from Ava, and I got it.

We sit in silence for a few minutes before I can meet his eyes. He has rounded eyes of sympathy, glassy with tears. A small smile is forced to his lips. "I'm so sorry I couldn't warn you, son. I wanted to tell you, but I feared you wouldn't listen. You had to learn for yourself. I hate to see the pain written on your face. I'm…sorry."

He doesn't move, but I get the energetic sensation of a hug. His compassion is my undoing. Tears form rivers down my face to puddle in my lap. "I forgive you. I know I wouldn't have listened anyway."

"You found your trouble, didn't you? Was it the girl?"

"Yeah," I whisper between croaks and sniffs. "I did. Ava triggers the nightmare where I relive the attack on the Antelope Bend. Only in the dream, the hand grabs me instead of Grandmother Winter. In the daytime, Ava is perfect for me. I want to spend every minute with her. However, I cannot live with someone who will haunt my dreams. Will you be there for me as I recover from her departure from my life?"

"Do you want to get rid of her? Son, I will stand by your every choice. That's the beauty of free will."

"What other choice do I have?" My treacherous heart dares to hope. I smash the feelings down. Hope is something for children who do not know how cruel the world can be. I would be a happier man if I never allowed myself to hold this pipedream.

"The problem seems to be Ava and the nightmare." He stomps in place to the cadence of his words. If I picked a bigger space, he may show me a sacred dance to get me out of this mess, but I added insult to injury as usual. When I mess up, I go big. I hang my head in my hands.

"So which would you like to get rid of—the nightmare or the girl?"

"Can I get rid of the nightmare?" My chin snaps in surprise, and I squint at him with suspicion. Nartan warned me his guides are tricky and speak in metaphors. My teacher doesn't move while I study him. His gentle smile and nonthreatening posture warm my heart. Hope blooms once more.

"You can, but it won't be easy. Once you forgive yourself, it will no longer have power over you."

"Forgive me? I can't be at fault—no disrespect— because I didn't kill anyone that day. I didn't burn down the village while Nartan was away. I didn't even fight. I ran and I hid. Do I need to forgive myself for hiding? What else was I supposed to do?" I plead to my teacher with my voice, my posture, and every fiber in my being. I don't blame myself for our banishment from the circle or any of the events leading up to it. What is he up to?

"Hiding was the best you could do at the time, so no one blames you for hiding. You need to forgive yourself for—"

Bang, bang, bang. "Ikshu, I can see the smoke coming out of the chimney flue. Come back to the teepee before you suffocate. If you pretend you aren't in there, you will find out I'm an excellent climber. I can have the flue blocked in seconds. If I must smoke you out like a hive full of bees, I will do it." Ava's voice thunders louder than her banging. I'm torn between listening to my teacher and preventing Ava from waking Nartan and Olive.

"Go to her, son. Keep the sacred space open, and I will watch over you. Your nightmares are done for tonight." A tingle of energy squeezes my shoulder in support and my teacher dissolves into smoke.

"Thank you, teacher," I whisper before extinguishing my pipe.

I yank open the door to a furious Ava. Her face is red with the cold of the weather and the heat of her temper. Her eyes flash with lightning while her lip curls into a snarl. Tiny fists rest at her sides as if I am about to be struck. The breeze tosses her hair like flames. The tendrils sparkle in the moonlight, adding to her mystical appearance.

"Well, what have you to say for yourself, Ikshu?"

"He's right. I don't ever want to let you go." The words fly out of my mouth on their own accord. I cram my fist into my mouth and await her reaction. The anger drains from her to puddle in the snow, soaking her slippers. The fire in her eyes mellows to a familiar storm cloud gray. She grabs my hand to pull me back to the teepee. Her determined stomping is adorable, as if she believes her delicate frame could drag mine anywhere I didn't wish to go.

"You are coming back to bed. You are telling me what made you leave. You are promising me never to abandon me again. Is that clear?" The whispered demands of the little tyrant are music to my ears.

She left the flap open to the teepee, so it is much cooler than when I left. She also left the covers open on the now frigid bed. She folds her arms in her protective posture and curls her shoulders forward. Her head hangs like a broken doll. Is she only cold or also hurt over my leaving? While she holds herself together, I knot the flap shut and hunt through the small woodpile for dry pieces. Luckily, I find a few sticks to put in the center fire pit, and they ignite easily.

I coax her closer, but she continues to shake. I hurt her. "Ava, it's not you—"

"Yes, it is. It's always me. What is it? I'm not sweet enough or curvy enough or…or…or…"

"You are everything I could ever wish for, but my past is in the way."

"Start talking," she studders through chattering teeth.

"Having your hands on me triggered a nightmare— that's not your fault. I have this nightmare often, but it was more intense because I wasn't alone. I could have hurt you. I went outside to—to—to—"

"Don't you dare try to lie to me, Ikshu. No one lies better than I do so I can detect them by instinct." Thank goodness her fire is returning. Angry Ava is manageable. Broken Ava may be more than my tender heart can bear.

"I went outside to call in my spiritual teacher for guidance."

"There," she says with a nod. "Honesty wasn't so hard, now was it?" She sits on the edge of the bed and shimmies out of the leggings. My eyes are glued to her silken flesh while my palms itch to touch her. Thankfully, she swings her bare limbs under the covers before I lose control of myself.

"It is almost five years now since our circle burnt to the ground. Almost everyone was killed…"

"I'm grateful you and Nartan survived, but mostly you. Please join me." She raises her arms to invite me to join her. Like a moth to a flame, I am drawn to her side. I sit but keep my back toward her. Her arms shake with nervous energy, so I don't cuddle her. I can't get cozy. What if I…

"I will watch over you tonight." My teacher's words echo in my mind. Instead of fear, they give me security. I swing my legs under the covers and lie back.

"When it all started, I was making a brush in Grandmother Winter's cabin. A white hand reached into the teepee and snatched her before my eyes. That hand is the creature of my nightmares. Your hands, as small and beautiful as they are, resemble my greatest fear." My words trail off. As her smile falls and takes my courage with it.

"So I can't touch you? Can I kiss you, or were those painful for you?"

"You misunderstand me." I clasp my hands around hers and kiss each knuckle. They are icy. I pull her closer and drape my arm over her shoulders. "When I'm awake, your touch brightens my world, but when I'm asleep, I am at the mercy of my past. I have a plan to work on it, so it isn't permanent…but…"

"—But you need sleeping space for the time being."

The air rushes out of my lungs when my worry releases it. She understands! She may be my soulmate after all. "Now you know why I have to sleep in the barn."

"Not happening."

"If you think it would be warmer in there, you are mistaken. It is a drafty structure. I would sleep in the cold for you."

"You aren't leaving until you prove my way doesn't work. I'm not giving up on you quickly. In fact, I may never give up on you." She crawls from the bed to the floor where she shivers with the icy contact. She grabs her bulky dress and piles of skirts discarded earlier. She twists, wrings, and bunches the clothes into a rope. The grunts she makes aren't ladylike as she works, but adorable in her way.

She secures the ends of the bundle with her hairpins and plops it down the center of the bed. I'm fascinated as she tucks the skins around it with gentle motions. She climbs into the space on the far side of her bolster. She disappears except for the coils of golden hair draped over the divide and her disembodied voice.

"There," she says when she settles. "Keeping men and women separated is an art form perfected by mothers-in-law all over the world. I read that some mothers-in-law stitch their sons-in-law between the blankets to keep him from touching her daughter before they were ready to have children. If this rope doesn't work, I'll let you sew me in. I can be like the mummies of Egypt in the book we were reading."

"You would sleep behind your skirts to stay with me?"

"Ikshu, you always manage to add a plot twist to our story. That's why I love being in your presence. Figuring this out will be our adventure." She snuggles into her blankets. "Goodnight, Ikshu."

"Sweet dreams, Ava." As the firelight dies, I thank the spirits of my ancestors for Ava's acceptance, my teacher's support, and the promise of another day.

Chapter 16

"You stayed." Breathless words of amazement leave my lips as soon as my eyes open. The dark circles under his eyes and lines by his mouth tell me he didn't sleep a wink. However, he is warm, dry, and by my side. That's a victory, right? I wouldn't have slept knowing he was in a cold, drafty barn all night at my expense.

"I stayed." His voice is groggy and deeper than usual. I shiver with delight. I would give up my featherbed covered with lacy quilts to awaken to his morning voice each day.

"Did you sleep at all?" I ask the back of his shoulders over my makeshift bolster. He sits up and looks ready to bolt. I don't know if I want the answer, but it will be better for us if I know the truth. Just because I have committed doesn't mean he has. Why buy the cow when you can get the milk for free? Not that I gave up any milk but only because he never asked.

"Rested enough to get you home safely. We can't risk doing this again. I can't be the one to ruin you. It would kill me inside." The look he gives me over his shoulder breaks my heart. The tenderness is more than I deserve. I may be Ava Wylder, but I have done nothing to warrant such sweetness. Guilt floods my insides. I'm playing a dangerous game with a man not made for risking his heart. If I had the strength in character of Ikshu, I would let him be. Too bad it only makes me want him more.

When I reach for him, he stands and steps away. I'm blinded by the light coming through the teepee flap when he opens the door. It is midmorning if the sun is reflecting off the newly fallen snow at this angle. I will be missed by now. With a sigh, I sit up and pull on the discarded leggings from last night.

I run my fingers through my hair until Ikshu hands me a brush. I scowl at my pins and decide to leave them here. *Torture devices.* Perhaps Ikshu will repurpose them someday into something as beautiful as what we could have. If only he were a gentleman in New York, we would be pushed together, and he would have no choice but to court me.

"If you don't want to wear the pins, would you like me to braid it for you? I…I saw the glare you gave them. I hope I never receive that look." He gives a half-hearted chuckle.

"There is nothing I want more right now." I turn my back to him, so I don't see his hesitation. Does he not respond to my advances because he is shy or wishes to reject me but can't because he is shy? He says he wants to be together but doesn't try to steal kisses. My experience with suitors is the opposite. What am I doing wrong? Doubts and questions tighten my gut, deciding for me to skip the pemmican for breakfast.

His answer is in his touch. Instead of dividing the blonde strands into three parts, he combs my hair from scalp to root. He gathers my hair in one calloused hand so the backs of his fingers caress my neck. The ends are wrapped around his fist as my scalp is treated to a massage. A noise of pleasure escapes my lips I swear I have never heard before. The rough fingertips of the other hand sweep behind, leaving tingles from my collar to my hairline. Why can't time stop so I can savor feeling alive?

He freezes when the sound of thundering hooves interrupts us. I hold my breath. One, two, one, two. The rhythm suggests it is only one horse, but it is approaching us at a high speed. "I believe you have a rescuer," he whispers. He drops my hair and the magic dissolves.

I want to scream in protest. This can't be over already. Tears fill my eyes while they plead with Ikshu to come back, to stop this, to change what is about to happen. The corners of his eyes are pinched, his frown heavy set, and the slump of his shoulders rounded inward. I recognize that posture. It is the cloak of defeat I wear often. One of us needs to fight. Today, I guess it's me.

I fly off the bed and out of the teepee into the snow. It slows me down, but I'm fueled by the angry swarm of hornets building in my belly. They sent me to New York alone for months to survive on my own. Why can't I make my own decisions in Wylder for a few days? Because I'm a lady? *Ha!* Wrong sister if they guessed who would respect that command.

Fletcher's duster flaps in the wind as his horse bucks at the base of Olive's cabin. He must have driven the horse too hard. He dismounts and drags the animal behind him. While I'm sorry he was worried, he obviously knew where I am because he's here now. His brown hair blows over his brow, letting his stormy brown eyes flash fire at me. *Good.* I'm itching for a fight, and I can take him on much easier than Finn with his guilt tactics, or Dad with his gentle lectures.

"Ava, where in tarnation have you been? What are

you wearing? How could you?"

"Here. This. Do what?" I stop just under his nose in anticipation of a brotherly spat.

"Don't be cute, Ava." He steps back to point his finger at me. "Dad was worried until Cyrus told us some townspeople saw you following a Native out of town. Dad asked his buddies at the saloon, who identified him as Ikshu. The whole town is talking about you, Ava. What have you to say?"

"The townspeople need more things to do than gossip about me." Ikshu stops behind me. His gentle energy cools the embers in my voice. He holds my coat open for me. I smile in gratitude before turning back to Fletcher. "Now that you have found me and verified that I'm not being held captive, you can report back to Dad."

"I don't think so, Ava." His glare at Ikshu could cut glass.

"I don't believe we have met," Olive says as she waddles down the porch steps of her cabin. She has one hand resting on her belly while the other is extended in friendship. "I'm Olive Sagebrush. Welcome to the Sagebrush Homestead."

One look at Nartan's menacing posture at the door of the cabin makes me grateful Olive is Fletcher's first point of contact. Subconsciously, I shrink into my folded-over posture and shift against Ikshu. His hand lifts to catch my elbow before I can lean on him fully. We connect. The contact is a brand through my coat. I gather his quiet security through the heat transfer and wear it like a blanket. Then I make the mistake of turning to Fletcher. His eyebrows connect to his hairline, eyes glued to the contact between us, and mouth agape.

"You must be Ava's brother. Are you Fletcher or

Finn? We didn't meet at the Christmas party as it was difficult for me to get around to all the groups of people," she says with a friendly chuckle and a pat to her belly. "Are you here to take Ava home? Nasty business getting snowed-in the way she did."

"Yeah, I'm Fletcher Wylder, and I'm here to take Ava where she belongs—"

"Who are you to say where I belong? Aren't you planning on shipping me off to New York as soon as possible? How can I belong at Wylder House when all the men there can't wait to see the back of me?" I screech the questions like a banshee while tears threaten to spill down my cheeks.

"Ava, now is not the time or place. You are supposed to be helping with Dad, not causing more trouble."

"Shows what you know! Dad doesn't want my help. He wants to spend time with his friends. There is no place for me with you—"

"—which is why you belong in New York!"

I risk my fragile confidence on a glance toward Ikshu. Why won't he say I belong with him? Here's his chance to speak up for me. Why doesn't he say something?

My heart skips a beat.

He never speaks.

He's Ikshu.

If he gave me one reason to believe in us, I would back him completely and get rid of my brother. My eyes search his face while Olive rambles at Fletcher to defuse the situation. Ikshu can't maintain eye contact. My heart sinks. I made my choice, so I must see it through for no other reason than my pride.

"Fletcher, I'm not going back to New York. I'm not returning with you now. You can throw a tantrum so loud it reaches from coast to coast, but I'm staying."

"Ava, don't push me. I want to save what's left of your reputation. You aren't thinking of your future." His face goes from red to purple with fury. If he doesn't stop grinding his molars, they will be stumps by the end of this conversation.

"I am, for once. Everyone saw me leave town yesterday as one of them. What will they say when I return the next day dressed like this? My reputation is better off with them guessing than confirming it with my presence." I fire the words at him with as much venom as I dare. He looks me up and down as if I just stepped into the snow. From my leather moccasins to my flowing hair, I look more untamed than Olive. Funny, my outsides finally match my insides, and he's looking at me as if I am a stranger.

"Oh, my lord, Ava. What have you done?"

"I have made choices for myself, Fletcher." Fletcher's focus moves from me to Ikshu. Steam billows from his nose. He clenches his fists and releases them with fury. He steps forward.

"Now I can assure you that nothing untoward has happened to your sister on our property, Mr. Wylder," says Olive, swinging her belly between Fletcher and Ikshu.

"Move out of my way. How can you—"

"That's enough." Nartan's commanding voice freezes everyone. The power coats me and I break out in goose-pimples. I bet he stopped time. Fletcher's rage melts from his face to a blank mask. Each step is an echoing crack as Nartan stomps down his stairs. Only the collective pairs of eyes move to watch him. "I don't appreciate the ruckus on my land caused by your guests, Ikshu. Mr. Wylder doesn't seem to want young Miss Wylder here, but she has voiced her wish to remain."

"She's my little sister…my youngest sister," Fletcher whispers. Even he doesn't have the nerve to raise his voice to Nartan.

"With all due respect, Mr. Sagebrush. I would like permission to spend more time here. I will be under your or Mrs. Sagebrush's supervision if you wish, but please don't make me go. Once I leave your land, I will be forced to go to New York." Something akin to compassion flashes across his face. It is so fast I would have missed it had I not been counting on it. He recognizes my predicament from when he and Ikshu were forced to start over in Wylder or go to the reservation. Being forced from the home where you always lived is a painful truth we share.

"I only wish you had pled your case when you first arrived, Miss Ava. I will provide a haven for you as long as I am allowed. Our family will get acquainted with yours in shelter from the elements. You will sleep in the cabin with Olive tonight if your visit spans the day. Does that meet with your approval, Mr. Wylder?"

"Absolutely not," Fletcher spits. It is as if Nartan lifted his spell long enough for those words to come out, only to shut down again. My brother freezes once more.

"Please voice your objections with less malice, Mr. Wylder. I am trying my best to clean up this mess which is not of my doing." Nartan's eyes flash with power above his sneer. I'm not sure Fletcher knows he is messing with a medicine man and how unwise that is. One glance at my brother shows he's terrified now. His fists tremble as his body vibrates with the urge to flee.

"Thank you, Mr. Sagebrush. I am grateful to spend the day with you. Have you had breakfast? Olive tells me you have a fondness for bear signs. If you have yeast handy, I can get a batch proofing in no time."

"She cooks?" Nartan's quiet question is directed at Ikshu more than me. Ikshu nods and looks at his shoes once more. I can't help but wish he would have contributed something to this conversation. It is not his way, but I'd like to think we are going to be a team. I hatch a plan to find out once and for all how much is my imagination and how much is mutual attraction.

"She bakes, dearest," Olive says with stars in her eyes. Nartan's stance softens at his wife's endearment. He smiles at her as if the rest of us melted into the snow. They gaze at each other while jealousy rakes its claws at my insides.

"This isn't over, Ava. I'll be back but not alone. I'm bringing Dad. I'm bringing Finn. I'm bringing the Sheriff." Fletcher mounts his horse and spits at my feet. "You, boy. Ikshu, is it? Ikshu, you will hang for this." He spurs his horse and gallops away, spraying all of us with snow.

"Nartan, Olive, Ikshu, I—"

"Turn for me. I need to look at the back of your tunic," Nartan commands.

My face pulls into puzzlement as I step in a circle and show him my plain tunic.

"Nartan, I didn't paint the wings of our tribe on her. We didn't do anything—"

Nartan cuts him off with a raised palm. "Ikshu, take the sheep to the forest to graze and then set up the loft in the barn for your sleeping quarters tonight. Looks like,

I'll be back in the teepee," Nartan huffs.

"Olive, please take our guest to the kitchen to make breakfast. I'd like something delicious to go with the explanation these two youngsters will be feeding us." He stomps toward the hen house. Like the closing of a book, the matter is settled and for today.

I'm free.

Chapter 17

"Spirits who are enlightened may stay. Spirits who are not enlightened must go, for I am creating a sacred space. Teacher, are you close?" The only good thing about being left in the cold, drafty barn after a day of being Nartan's slave is I have unfettered access to his spiritual tools. The wooden shutters blow open, allowing a cloud of fat snowflakes to enter. The flakes grow as they descend into the warm stalls instead of shrinking as they warm. They swirl around the four horses before settling on the milking stool in the corner. Lady dances nervously until FoolsGold swipes his nose along her neck.

The flakes coalesce into the familiar shape of my aged teacher. The tunic fits better than the last time I saw him, and he stands straighter. Instead of the usual walking stick, he leans on a spear adorned with a red feather, strands of beads, and a flint arrowhead. While still leathery with age, the lines in his face are suggestions rather than the carvings he once wore. White feathers stick up from the braid at the back of his head. The slow burn of envy travels down my spine at the sight of those feathers.

"I have arrived for the war, son. Are you ready?"

"You might be a little late. Fletcher already came and left. Ava fought for us, but I couldn't open my mouth…as usual."

"Those Wylder boys have yet begun to fight for the virtue of their troublesome sister. However, that is none of my concern. I'm in this realm to guide you. Tonight, we fight for your voice. If you have decided Ava is the reward you wish to receive."

"Keep Ava forever? How?"

"Hasn't Nartan drilled into your head, whatever you say will manifest? Especially in the presence of a spirit guide?"

"Manifest? Okay," I say, rolling the idea around in my head. "I will be able to say what I want in front of the enemy…whoever they may be."

"Let's get started before the trouble interrupts," Teacher says.

"How? What trouble? Should I get Nartan?"

"No, if he needs to intervene, he will know. Funny thing about Nartan, it isn't having the courage to intervene but the wisdom to let things take their course is where he struggles. Lie on the ground, son, close your eyes, and lend your spirit to Mother Earth."

I lie down and spread my limbs into a star-shape. I breathe deeply and concentrate on making myself as heavy as possible. I have no idea what he means by lending my spirit. Having as much connection with the ground as possible is a good start, right?

Then it hits me.

Tendrils of energy soak through my skin and wrap themselves in coils around my organs. The pull of gravity increases until the weight on my chest threatens to choke me. The pressure in my head increases. A strange stinging sensation creates a crown the circumference of my head, lifting above my ears. The same sting itches the palms of my hands as they rest on the dirt floor.

"Hold steady, son," Teacher says tersely. "She's got your spirit. All is as it should be. Breathe in the trust and love from the universe."

In, out. In, out. It takes all my strength to calm my galloping heart into a serene rhythm. The stinging in my palms travels up my arms. When it meets at my chest, a fire is kindled, and a gentle warmth fills my heart with love. Tears prick the corners of my eyes when the feelings of compassion and kindness register. The stinging ruins the bliss from the connection and travels between my collar bones to my neck. My throat closes. I fight to breathe calmly.

"Trust it. Don't fight it."

"I'm trying," I croak. My vocal cords seize. A strange fluttering sensation sends squeaks and coughs from my mouth.

"This isn't the worst yet, son. Sleep is on its way. Just know I am here. You are not facing this alone."

"Facing wh—" My words are cut off by the stinging.

I'm in Grandmother Winter's teepee when I sit up. She is perched on a stump and sewing at lightning speed with gnarled fingers. Every few stitches, she smiles at a little boy struggling to thread a brush. I step behind her to see a younger version of myself. I wasn't as talented as I thought back then. My tongue is over my lips in concentration, but my fingers will not obey. The brush slips from my grasp and clatters on the ground with every tuck. With the wisdom of the owl, Grandmother lets me find my way.

The hoofbeats from my nightmares start their staccato rhythm. "No, Teacher!" My adult form yells for mercy. I'm in my nightmare…twice. My child form doesn't react to the sound, but Grandmother sits up. She looks to my adult self but doesn't see me. She leans forward and back as if to find the source of my shout. I must be in a different part of the spirit plane. My alert allows her to hear the hooves, and she places a hand over the brush. She whispers her warning to my child likeness.

"You are on another timeline, Ikshu. We are on a journey to heal you. The event which took your voice is almost here. See how your spirit alerted the magic in her. She knew to save you. Your child self had a destiny, and now she knows it. She also knows she is to die."

"NO!"

"Ikshu, it is the way of the Creator, and we are not to argue. You have a purpose to bring to the world, and she saw it. She did the best she could, and now you must learn you did too."

A thump sounds at the top of the teepee. A lighted stick lays across the top. The leather ignites quickly with red hot cinders raining on us. My child self wakes from his concentration and panic pulls his mouth and eyes wide open. He jumps up and grabs Grandmother by the elbows. He pulls so hard her shoulders buckle. "Come, Grandmother, we must leave. Something about this fire scares me. Please let's go," the little voice cries.

"No, no, no," my adult self cries. Tears flow into rivers down my face. My limbs tremble and my shoulders curl. My spine bows and I howl with impotent rage. "I can't live this anymore. I don't deserve this."

My child self screams as the white hand reaches in. I reach for the hand to stop it. The hand is smaller than mine. I could crush it. I hear my own evil laughter echo through the teepee. Yes, I'll crush it, then I will crush the owner.

"No, no, no, Ikshu," Grandmother whispers. She is looking at my spirit. My thoughts freeze. She sees me. She sees the plan unrolling in my head. The hand grabs at air and disappears.

"You cannot alter this timeline, Ikshu. We aren't at the event." My teacher's counsel is miles away as I stare at Grandmother Winter. She smiles at my teacher with a toothless grin. She mouths at him, and he puts his hand over his heart.

"You mustn't speak. You must not let them find you. Promise me you will be silent as you crawl out of the back of the teepee. Promise!" she yells at my child self while shaking me by the shoulders.

"Teacher, she never said we. In my nightmares, she always said we must be silent as we escape. Why is this time different?"

"Son, she never said we at the time. You manufactured her words so you could blame yourself for her death. This is your life-altering event. I am so sorry."

"Teacher, she recognizes you. She accepted her death when she saw you. What is going on?"

"Ikshu, when you see your true love, don't you follow her?" His breath hitches as she is yanked from the teepee by the pale hand. Oh no. My teacher is Grandfather Winter who died before I was born. I have heard hours of tales about his bravery, wisdom, and his undying love for Grandmother.

"Next, we must make your conquering event to fix this, son. We—"

The image fades, and I'm back in the barn. Is that my head pounding?

****

Olive's snores are music to my ears. Despite sitting all day while I waited on her, she fell asleep instantly. Another stroke of luck is she chose to sleep next to the wall, leaving me closest to the door. I would have never had the nerve to climb over her to get out of this bed. Time to do what I do best…sneak out. Without a bar as a close neighbor, I can leave the door unlocked for a fast return. No way am I trusting those creaky stairs not to alert Nartan. I'm out and vaulting over the side of the porch in no time flat.

I don't trust the open spaces between the vats either. The moon isn't full, but the shadow I cast would cover half the yard. I tiptoe past the chicken coop and through the vegetable garden. Slush and mud coat my moccasins and leggings. I hope they dry out before I must return to bed. Olive may think she's sleeping with a pair of giant worms.

I slog my way through the forest, leaving a trail of disturbed snow in my wake. My nighttime trek will be discovered in the morning, but my plan will be completed by then. Shallow breathes, soft footsteps, and careful foot placement so no one hears. I weave through the trees past the soaking vats, the outhouse, the smokehouses, and finally Ikshu's teepee.

The barn has a ten-foot clearing between it and the tree line. I've come so far but I'm starting to lose my resolve. Is Ikshu awake? There is smoke escaping the open window at the top of the barn. It could be a trick of the moonlight, but I believe there is a candle alight inside. What if he doesn't answer? What if he sends me away in humiliation? I'm rooted against the last tree and holding it for dear life. As safe as I feel, I can't stay here to be discovered by Nartan. I lift my tunic to my waist to give my legs a longer reach.

3...2...1...

I kick up snow in all directions as I sprint to the barn. The white powder swirls around me like a shield of protection as I hustle. I bang on the doors as loudly as I dare. They rattle and shake, but there is no movement inside I can detect. I bend to look through the door jam. Ikshu lays in the middle of the floor. The glow from his pipe reflects off the sheen of his sweat-coated chest. He is twitching with limbs flopping while he moans in agony. My heart jumps. I must save him from his nightmare!

How to get in? The door is firmly locked. The stall windows are latched as well. I wander around the barn, running my hands over the walls in vain. The gaps between the planks are not large enough for my fingers to fit through. Why can't there be a loose slat when I need one? I thump my back against the barn in frustration. There is a square on the ground where light has melted the snow. Sure enough, there is a path of ragged boards to the open window at the top of the barn.

Over my years at school, I have learned the hardest part of sneaking out is not the sneaking part. The most difficult thing is to find your way back inside. Before I was confident enough to return through the front door, I left unlocked, I practiced climbing up the side of the old manor home which housed the female residents. Climbing that house was a challenge because the thatched siding was whitewashed until it shined in the latest New York fashion. This barn with its numerous rounded crossbeams and uneven runner planks will be a breeze.

I clear the snow off my shoes with my hands.

Stepping on the lowest crossbeam, I walk until I'm a few feet off the ground at the junction of the X. Had they taken the time to sand off the bark and square the beams, I may have struggled a little. Who am I kidding? They left the beams twice the width of my feet, wasting valuable wood. I step over the cross and continue my tentative stroll until I come to the horizontal brace. The junction of the next X is a foot or so above my head, so I reach high. My fingers gain purchase, and I'm in business. Within minutes, I'm at the window and swing my leg over the side without hesitation. My brother's heads would spin like tops if they saw how quickly I could scale a three-story barn. I'm pretty amaz—

I dump myself over the side and enter with a crash. How did this window get open if there is no loft on this side of the barn? Wiggle fingers, wiggle toes, I'm good. Luckily for me, I land on the Sagebrush family's winter haystack. Had I tried this any other month, I would have been severely injured. My wiggling dislodges my perch and I slide down the hay to the dirt.

"Ava, Ava, Ava," Ikshu chants my name as he rushes to my side. "What are you doing? Where did you come from?" His bewildered look is adorable. He tests my arms and legs for motility while I bask in the sensation of his hands running over my body.

"Well, my work here is done. I wanted to save you from your nightmare, and you are awake now." I give him a half-hearted smile. How can I say I snuck out to seduce him into making me his wife? How can I entice him with feminine grace when I just crashed through the window? I bet I have a grass nest embedded in my hair. I pat my head gently to dislodge an errant blade, only to find I have an equal amount of hair and straw tucked into my braids. I can't help but giggle. My giggles turn to laughter which escalates into hysterics.

"I wish you hadn't awoken me. I was working on my voice and not focused on the physical world. You could have been killed and I would have been too far away to save you." His somber words cool my laughter. I sit up with a hiccup.

"Ikshu, I don't know what tomorrow will bring and I wanted one last night with your magic."

"My magic?"

"The way I feel when I'm here is magical. It is the opposite of how I feel in New York which is where my brothers will send me. I have a feeling tomorrow will be my last day in Wylder unless something changes. Something big," I say. I hope he takes the hint. We sit listening to the horses' shuffle, the wind batting the upper window's shutters about, and the beating of our hearts.

I can't wait any longer. I untie the laces at the side of my tunic at the bottom, removing the leather ties up my waist to just under my arm. Ikshu watches my hands until the first inches of my belly are exposed.

Then he jumps back like I've lit myself on fire. "What are you doing, Ava?"

"I'm creating my story. I need some of your magic to take back with me."

"Ava, no. Stop. Ava," he protests with his hands up. I unknot the ties on the sleeve. The tunic hangs at an angle across my body. The slightest tremble and I would shake it to the floor.

"Turn this adventure into a love story, Ikshu."

"I can't, Ava," he snaps. He puts his hands on my shoulders to secure the tunic in place. Tears well into my eyes. I guess this attraction is all my imagination. My chest hollows with grief, and I struggle for air. Twin rivers flow down my face. "Ava, I can't be your toy. I am not built to be the man who ruins you so you can stay in Wylder. I don't know what I did to give you the impression I could. I'm not going to be the person you manipulate to get out of schooling in New York. I sympathize with you, but I am powerless."

He leans forward to place a chaste kiss on my forehead. I hold him hostage by pressing my forehead against his when he tries to withdraw. I clasp my hands over his and hold back my sobs. "You are right. It isn't fair that I ruin your reputation in town just to ruin my own. I won't tell a soul. You have the power to turn this adventure into a love story for me to take back. Why can't you make love to me?"

"If I make love to you, it will consume me. I won't be able to let you go. That's the problem. I have nothing to offer you but want you all the same."

"That's not true. You have open land and freedom."

"I have a hard life of year-round working. Feel the callouses on my hands. They aren't from studying all day like you suitors. Do you really want these rough hands to touch you? You will be trading a life of books for a life of tanning hides."

"Ikshu, look at my hands. They are small, fair, and completely useless. Those New York suitors you like to compare yourself to have the same hands as me. If I wanted those hands to touch me, I would touch myself and cut out the stupid courtship exercises. Do you see this?" I point to a red spot at the base of my middle finger on my right hand.

He cups my palm in his hands and kisses the spot. A

blush creeps up my arm. It is followed by the fire that dances over my skin whenever he touches me. "I got this spot rolling biscuit dough for Olive today. I have never had a better day in the city. Olive told me stories about her travels all over the country. Did you know she went from tribe to tribe learning all the stories? She talked while I made enough hot rocks to feed Jake's on a Sunday, and I bet half of them are gone."

"See, your days will be slaving over a hot stove—"

"And I will love it. Do you think I could write her stories into a book? Do you know how happy that would make me? How about when her babies are born? I will get to help because Olive says she will have more than one child this spring. I won't even have to take turns with someone."

"Are you sure this is what you want?"

There is no turning back. I pull the tunic over my head and challenge him. I resist the urge to squirm as he looks from my waist slowly back to my face. "I'm certain. Are you?" The words are whispered but hang between us like a morning fog. I count my heartbeats while placing his palms over my breasts. His throat undulates to swallow his fear for me. I know what I'm doing, but he hasn't a clue. I must stay in control during his gentle exploration of my most secret treasures or I will scare him away.

Hesitantly, he twitches his fingers to test my softness. I loosen my grip on his right hand when his courage fuels its movement. Time slows. I watch his face for rejection, but desire threatens to scorch me. I must rely on my skin to catalog the movement of his fingers for I am ensnared in his gaze. His knuckles trace along the underside of my breast on a meandering path to my collar. Their journey follows the bone to the little hollow at the center. His palm flattens to grip my neck at the delicate place where it meets my shoulders. He is memorizing me.

With a surge of energy, his hands are tangled in my hair and gliding along my scalp. I wait for the hesitant kisses I have come to associate with him. I'm overjoyed when he pulls my body across his lap. His lips claim mine in a whirlwind of passion. I open my mouth to breathe, and it becomes an invitation for his tongue to brand me. He tilts my head to deepen the kiss, and I drown in the fiery love he pours down my throat.

My stimulated breasts are smashed against the hard planes of his muscles. My greedy hands memorize the planes and valleys of his back and arms. If nothing else, I will have this experience to fuel my imagination for the rest of my life. If I must marry one of those coddled boys in New York, I will have the body of a real man mapped in my mind and burnt on the tips of my fingers. I rub swirls with my palms over his pectoral muscles, down his abs, and hit what must be his belt buckle.

His groan indicates I hit something else entirely.

****

This is moving too fast and spiraling out of control. The little minx has stripped my self-control and scattered it on the floor with her tunic. She is making a mistake, but I am too weak to save her. The fallen angel of my wildest fantasies has an adventurous side beyond riding into the sunset. She never claimed to be a good girl, and her wandering hands show me why.

"Ava, have you thought about what happens after this?" I struggle to get the words out between her aggressive kisses. Common sense says to push her away.

I'm twice her size, but her power over me is irrational. My hands are glued to her ribcage where her breasts caress my thumbs with her every movement. Her skin is so soft I fear I will snag it with my brutish treatment of her.

She pulls back to look into my eyes but holds my shoulders captive with her tiny hands. "The best outcome is I get the lifetime of adventure I always wanted. The worst outcome is I go where I'm supposed to be, which will please my family." She breathes each word between short breaths. The subtle green in her stormy eyes has deepened with desire so they glow like the eyes of a forest spirit. Her lips are swollen with my kisses. "My only thoughts are how far I want to go tonight, Ikshu. Tomorrow's events don't interest me."

I lean forward to kiss the determined look off her face. Doubts swirl in my gut about what she is determined to have. A life of her choosing or a life of her choosing *with me*. I would certainly give her anything she wanted if she were mine, but I need her to want me for me first. The protests lodge in my throat in a familiar vise. She takes the lead when I hesitate and lunges at me. We tumble off the bottom slope of the haystack, and I end up flat on my back. She lands on me with an adorable "*oomph*."

The fall doesn't slow her commanding hands but adds her legs to our tangle of passion. The squeeze of her thighs at my hips is too much. She is suspended inches above contact but is already threatening to be a scorching paradise. I ball my hands into fists at her back to resist pressing her down.

As I fight my instincts, she goes into a frenzy of need. Her hands flutter over my sheepskin leggings like butterflies as she tugs, grips, and pulls at the unrelenting leather. Our bodies are engorged with heat and coated with sweat which has fused the material to our bodies. She breaks our kiss and slides to sit on my outstretched legs to focus on taking off my leggings. I sit up to stop her or help her. I'm lost to know which plan I am following.

Our eyes meet.

We laugh.

Deep belly-quaking laughter fills the barn and echoes into the night. Her laughter is music more beautiful than the first birds of spring. It curls itself in the darkest part of my heart, bringing light to my darkest corners.

"Ikshu, I can't pull your pants off," she says between giggles. She rolls with laughter until she is curled into a ball at my side.

Something inside me clicks into place. I need her. My objectives shift from protecting her from herself to giving her everything she wants. Her laughter claims my heart and soul. I want to be the hero I see shining in her eyes when she gazes at me. Maybe for tonight, I can be her everything…even if the world takes it away in the morning. I promise myself to love her more than she can stand…but not on the floor and not rushed like this.

When I stand up, I have her tiny frame in my arms. My chest warms when she coils her arms around my neck. She lays her head on my chest in total trust and her golden hair glides over my arm with each step. I climb the stairs to the loft on the opposite side of the barn from where she burst inside. I have made a nest of buffalo skins for the night. With reverence, I lay her on the makeshift bed and spread her hair over my pillow. She doesn't protest as I spread her legs from their curled position.

"When your temperature rises, the leather molds to you like a second skin of protection. The spirit of the animal is protecting you from the work or fighting which overheated you. You must let them know they can let down their guard by rolling them inside out. The leather will encase the spirit to release you." My voice is more of a growl than a whisper. A quiet strength lurks beneath the surface that was never there before.

I watch her face for protests and silently beg for acceptance as I slip my fingers under the waist of her leggings. With each inch I roll down her body, a flush grows under her chin to cover her breasts. When I reach her ankles, I slide the attached moccasins off her feet. I rub her cold arches in my palms. Then I rub circles up her legs to memorize every inch of my Ava before she returns to her side of the tracks.

****

He stands over me to undress with a commanding presence I have never felt around him. My heart threatens to burst from my chest with anticipation. Who is this man, and how I am lucky enough to be in his bed? I never want to leave and say a prayer he feels the same. I would ask, but I fear breaking the spell over him. So I'm silent. I don't dare blink as his hands travel down his legs to roll his legging to the floor. He's magnificent, and tonight…he's mine.

He crawls up my body to blanket it with his own. My head is caged in by his muscular arms which hold his weight from crushing me. "Sweet, beautiful, untamed, fallen angel, I'm asking one last time, are you sure? Do you choose me?"

"Love me, Ikshu."

"Ava, I already do."

Chapter 18

"Ikshu, I'm so glad to find you up and dressed. Olive is beside herself. We have a problem." Nartan's brow is furrowed with worry on his wife's behalf. At one time, it bothered me, but now I get it. When Ava and I have our relationship cemented, I will move heaven and earth to suit her moods. I may have to today. Our relationship rests on shaky ground, but our cord has been tied.

"Olive is so sorry, but she lost Ava. Your guest must have slipped out during the night. Who knows where she is now?"

Wow, the little minx managed to sneak past Nartan on his land. My eyebrows lift sky-high, and laughter threatens to burst from me. "No worries, brother. She is up in the loft. She has been here with me." I keep my tone light and nonthreatening.

"Her brothers are on their way and possibly with the Sheriff. Ikshu, what have you done?"

"Keep it down. She's still asleep. When she wakes, we will decide how we wish to proceed."

"Wait for her to wake while her brothers are on their way? Have you lost your mind? They will hang you for deflowering their sister whether anything happened in here last night or not. How will we proceed? You have no clue what is about to happen. They will take one look at your hair, your clothes, your home, and cart you to the gallows.

"We either rush Ava back to the cabin with Olive or you run!" My brother paces as he reads me the riot act. The words tumble out at a breakneck rate of speed. His fingers tear at his hair until it escapes his braids to form an angry black cloud.

Clump, clump, clump. By the tempo of the hoofbeats, I would guess four horses are traveling down our road. They are at a gallop but not the dangerous speed of Fletcher's approach yesterday. "It is too late to hide, Nartan. We will face her family—"

"I can still hitch your horse. You could run to the reservation. The tribe could shelter you. If you promised not to leave the reservation, maybe the Wylder family would let you be. Olive and I would visit often—"

"I'm not running. You taught me to stand for my beliefs no matter the trouble they bring. Thank you for your offer, but I'm taking responsibility. You know it's my way, Nartan."

"And why I choose to be with him." Ava's voice floats from the second floor like a song from the heavens. She leans over the railing, and her hair reaches down to me. The golden strands catch the morning sun to shine brighter than its rays. I made the brush that rests in her hand. I made the clothes that sit on her body. I placed the glow on her face too. Male satisfaction warms my belly and curls the corners of my lips into a smile. She's my choice too. Will I be able to say it when the time comes?

****

I'm sure my family would be more comfortable had I changed into my dress before approaching them, by the looks on their faces. Their heads did a slow sweep of my leather attire in unison before scowls adorn their brows. I didn't even pin up my hair. I've changed. I'm staying.

The sooner they stand with me, the easier the transition will be.

"Welcome to our homestead, gentlemen. Fletcher, I have met, but will you introduce me to your friends?" Olive waddles down the stairs of her cabin to meet my family members clustered at her front door.

Cousin Branch dismounts his horse to shake her outstretched hand. Dad is slower but makes the effort to greet her. My rude brothers stay on their horses and glare down their noses at her. The gesture ignites a fire in my belly. If Nartan doesn't smite them for the slight, I may box their ears on Olive's behalf.

"Sorry to intrude like this, Mrs. Sagebrush," says Dad. "It seems our little Ava has gotten herself into mischief again. Thank you for looking out for her and keeping her safe in the snowstorm. I was beside myself with worry when she didn't come home. I had no idea where she was and thought it best to involve her brothers."

He means well but paints me as a ten-year-old who followed a butterfly into the woods. "Well, you see plainly I am fine. Fletcher saw that yesterday. If he had told you I was content, it would have saved you the ride out here in the cold." I shoot daggers at Fletcher with my eyes. I roamed around New York without their concern. Why is Wylder so different?

"You aren't fine, and we brought the Sheriff to take care of it," Finn says in his no-nonsense tone. I look to Dad for support and come up empty. I guess I will be fighting this battle on my own.

"Ma'am, I don't believe we have met. I'm Branch Wylder. Sheriff Hanson is retiring, and I will be taking on the role of Sheriff later this month." My insides crumble at his words. Cousin Branch is the next Sheriff of Wylder? With the power of a Sheriff at their backs, my brothers can make me do anything they want. I might as well start walking to the train station now.

"Howdy, Sheriff. I'm Olive Sagebrush, and the tall guy walking out of the barn is my husband, Nartan. This is his younger brother, Ikshu. If you ever need a gun holster, tobacco pouch, leather duster, or fur-lined snow boots, Ikshu is your guy. He's the finest craftsman in Wylder, and we tan the leather right here on our homestead." I can't tell if my cousin's smile is genuine or if he's humoring Olive, but she brings down the temperature of the situation by half. When Olive nods behind me to indicate Ikshu, I sneak a glance at him. His complexion has gone white as a ghost.

"Now that everyone knows each other and knows we are all friendly, I will see you at home later. Olive, let's go inside and whip up some breakfast," I announce with a clap of my hands. I leave the safety of Ikshu's warmth to cross the gauntlet to Olive's side. I loop my arm through her elbow on my way to the cabin stairs. They may want to puff themselves up like hens, but as far as I'm concerned, this conversation is over.

"Not so fast, Ava," Finn says. I am jerked back when Olive doesn't follow me. She gives me the smallest headshake. She is asking me to help her defend her men. I understand the position I have put the Sagebrush family, but my family would never hang someone over harboring me in a snowstorm. They don't know the extent to which I have committed myself to Ikshu, and the longer we stand here freezing, the more likely I am to accidentally blurt it out.

"Ava, sweetheart, in your absence, we talked about

your future. We decided your visit to Wylder needs to end. In light of this, it was agreed I am not a suitable guardian for a young lady who needs the social circles of a bigger city…" My treacherous father cannot meet my eyes. His lecture trails off into the snow. How dare he allow my brothers to railroad him!

"What Dad is saying is I have too many responsibilities to watch you. The store, the house, the horses, Dad, it is all too much. I need to know you are safe—"

"—you mean out of your hair. Finn Wylder, I have asked repeatedly to work in the store and to have more responsibilities with the house. Dad, how many suppers did I throw out because you wanted to play cards and eat at the saloon? You never gave me a chance." Tears choke my throat, but I continue with a shaky voice. "At this homestead, I have a purpose. Those pies I baked which made you feel trapped were appreciated by Olive."

"Guys, it seems like Cousin Ava came here on her own volition. I can't bring up Ikshu on charges of kidnapping when he didn't drag her here. Even the witnesses claim she followed him without his knowledge."

Witnesses? They have gone around town, asking the local gossips about me to arrest Ikshu. My fury builds to where I bet steam comes from my ears. Olive starts to cry and Nartan rushes to her side. She removes my arm from her elbow to nestle in the comfort of his embrace. His expression over the top of her head is murderous. I need to get control of this situation before it turns ugly. My eyes plea with Ikshu to say something. Here is his opening. Why won't he stand up for us?

"I can assure you my brother is not the aggressor in

the relationship between Miss Wylder and himself. You can ask anyone in town, and they will say he's gentle to a fault. Please do not condemn a man who wishes to make a quiet living but attracted the attention of a young girl." Nartan's voice is hypnotic with its deep rumbles reaching for my innermost thoughts. Power radiates from him, but his calm facade stays in place.

"No one is blaming Ikshu...yet," Fletcher says. "We know our sister would do anything to run wild with no responsibilities. It is not his fault she saw him as a means to avoid going back to school. He could have been any man."

"That's not true!" I sob the words and lose control over myself. How could they think so little of me? It is too late when I look at Ikshu. The idea of my using him as a toy was already there. My brother's statement confirms it. If he ruins my chance at happiness, I'll never forgive him. "If you force me on the train, I will never come back. I will have no reason to come back." My tears drip down my tunic. The vertical streaks create prison bars across my chest.

"Ava, please, it is not like that. We love you and want what is best for you. The life you could have in New York is more than I can give you here. Just give it a chance." My father's pleas sound ridiculous. It is like he hasn't listened to a word I have said. I gave city life a chance for years. He has ignored all my complaints about the noise, the smells, and the suitors in New York. Something inside me curdles like spoiled milk.

"Give it up, Ava," Finn says. "You had your dramatic adventure. You are done. It is time for you to grow up. You need a husband, and you won't find one out here, hiding on the Sagebrush Homestead."

****

Sheriff Wylder's hand looks identical to the one in my nightmare. I can't stop staring at it. The longer fingernails, the pattern of wrinkles across the knuckles, the shape, and the bright white of his hand trigger a visceral response in my gut. He's the new Sheriff. Another Wylder. The four men are cut from the same bolt of cloth. They own everything and have the hands of my worst nightmare. As much as I love Ava, I haven't the strength to keep her. My trauma is getting in the way again.

It is a sign I should let her go. Why does the thought threaten to choke the life from me? She could find someone of her station to spoil her. She's a shining light who could bring anyone to love her. How long would it take for her to get over me if she is miles away? I struggle for air as the hole in my chest combines with the tightening of my throat.

They continue to argue, and I zone out when Nartan steps in. He towers over the other men and glares down his nose. Nartan always does the right thing because he is spiritually guided. He will get them to leave because he will protect our homestead. He wants a quiet, peaceful life, and having the family who owns the town angry on our doorstep is counterproductive. I concentrate on breathing and leave this fight in Nartan's care. The world stops spinning, and my nausea backs away a touch. One more breath and my nightmares are firmly hidden in the back of my mind. It is safe for me to take control from my brother.

Ava is crying and screaming like an evil spirit. Olive is crying too but tucked under Nartan's arm as he reasons with the Wylders. I did this. I couldn't stop thinking about Ava's cold feet and impractical shoes after the Christmas party. Something in me needs to protect her and provide her comfort. I wish I could wrap my arms around her now and dry her tears, but she is busy fighting for us.

She's doing the job I should be doing if I want to prove I could be her husband. My mouth moves, but there is no sound. I curse my teacher for not restoring my voice last night. All he did was give me another nightmare and reveal his identity. He probably reclaimed his wife's soul too. I was manipulated to reunite them for eternity. Someone got their soulmate. Shouldn't it have been me? I clear my throat. Even that is silent.

"Give it up, Ava," the graying version of Fletcher says. "You had your dramatic adventure. You are done. It is time for you to grow up. You need a husband, and you won't find one out here hiding on the Sagebrush Homestead."

Ava's gaze on my face burns hotter than the sun. She needs her rescue. Here is my chance to ask for her hand. "Just say the word, Ikshu. If I need to go to the reservation to get a tattoo like Olive's forehead, I want to do it. What will it take Ikshu? Tell them I'm yours." She whispers the words to me as if there is no one else around. How does she have the power to make people disappear? When it is the two of us, I can speak freely for she chases the demons in my head away. I cannot let this fallen angel slip through my fingers.

My mouth opens to respond, but no sound emerges. I try again only to achieve a squeak. I fight through the images of my nightmares blending with the images of her family standing around me. I have one foot on the ground and the other in my nightmare. Their hands catch my gaze and tear my focus from Ava. I want to stay present, but my mind fights it. Inhaling I build my strength.

"Save it, Ikshu. Ava is using you to get out of school. She would drop you before she reaches the altar." Her brother is giving me an exit. He thinks I'm trying to put her down easily when I fail to speak my mind. He doesn't understand because I haven't said how much I love Ava. I need to say it. Here is my chance at happiness.

"But I love her" thunders through my mind, but my mouth doesn't get the message. Time stops as I struggle to transfer the information through my head. I open my lips to the correct shape to exhale the first letter sound in vain.

Branch puts up his hands to stop me. His palm is inches from my nose. It blocks out everything else in my field of vision. I'm no longer in the open but stuck in a smoke-filled teepee. Instead of the arguing of Ava with her family, my ears fill with the screams of the dead. Bile roars up my system threatening to burn off my tongue. My body sways. My mind spins. Then everything goes black.

Chapter 19

"Go away," I yell at my teacher. "I didn't summon you. When I needed you, you were worse than absent! You lead me to believe I could have something worth living for and someone to share it with. You promised my voice, and somehow it only works when I'm with you. Is that some limit you forgot to tell me?"

"Son, I'm so sorry for the trouble that girl caused you—"

"Ava. Her name is Ava. She is Miss Ava Wylder. She's the little princess of this town, and everyone seems to know it but me…and you." I throw my hand up to him in dismissal. As much as Nartan complains about not being able to summon his guides, my teacher comes and goes as he pleases.

"I warned you Ava is nothing but trouble. However, she is the catalyst to get you to release your trauma. If we can repeat the healing, I can—"

"No, no, no," I say with vigorous head shaking. "I went into my nightmare with you to be good enough for Ava. There is nothing in it for me now because she's leaving town. I didn't have the voice to ask her to stay. I froze. Instead, I will live the quiet life my brother is always touting for him. He will raise a family and enjoy the love of his life for me. Find someone else to teach. I'm a lost cause."

"I refuse to give up, and don't you dare disrespect

me the way you disrespect your teacher." Nartan's voice shakes the poles holding my teepee together. It shrinks to half the size when he enters. I can't believe we used to live in here together. His calumet hangs from his bottom lip despite its large size. He crosses his arms over his chest and nods to my teacher. Behind him trails the six Water-Pouring Men. "I called your teacher with my team. We are going to heal you together. I let you fight this battle on your own long enough. It is time for me to step up as your leader, your medicine man, and most of all, your brother."

"Nartan, please let me be miserable for a while. I don't have the strength for this. My heart is aching. I promise to call upon you when I'm back to myself or at least to a version of myself who wants to be healed."

"Son, this will always haunt you if you do not release it. Imagine being able to sleep through the night. I'm still committed to helping you. I want to give you a better life." My teacher's expression is destroyed with grief. As he speaks, I take in his appearance. He stands straight without a walking stick. His frame has filled with lean muscle which fits the tunic he wears. The thin wisps of hair have grown to a silver mane which hangs in two braids over his ears. It seems the worse I feel, the better he looks.

"I am learning to accept my fate." I plop onto my bed and my head bangs against Ava's petticoat barrier. Teacher kneels at my feet and leans his face into my view.

"This will keep you from giving your heart to the next girl. You will be stuck—"

"I already can't give my heart to the next girl. My heart is leaving with Ava as if she has packed it in her trunk. She's on a train traveling toward men brave enough to claim her." I jump up and pace. I rake my fingers through my hair before shaking the weakest strands onto the floor. Tears leave my eyes as I lay my innermost secrets at their feet.

"I don't blame the men who want her. She's too beautiful. Her insides shine like the morning sun to make anyone near her feel alive. I sit here knowing she's about to make some man the happiest man on earth. His spirit will rise to heights he never imagined, just by being hers." I pause for breath and punch the canvas. It undulates at me in mockery.

"You know what will happen next? He will touch her. He will touch my Ava, and I must sit back and take it because she needs to be touched. He won't love her as much I do, but he will be the one touching her."

"There could be another girl—" My teacher risks my wrath only because my fists would sail through his ghostly form.

"That doesn't matter," I wail. "I'm dead inside. No one can live without a heart. I was stupid to believe otherwise. Leave me alone."

"No." My brother's voice cuts me to ribbons. I openly sob and fall to my knees. "What are the chances of stopping the train in Wylder long enough to heal Ikshu?"

"Train ain't arrived yet, chief. It's difficult to stall it in Wylder when it's stuck in Ogden, Utah," says one of his spirit guides. Their snickers fill the teepee.

"Terrible business in Ogden, Utah, chief. A sinkhole opened up and gobbled the track the way your wife gobbles pie." Nartan's spirit guides laugh and pat each other on the back. He smiles at them, but it isn't a happy smile. It's a scary smile.

"Ikshu, son, I am asking for your permission to enter your nightmare again. I am bringing all the arrows in our quiver this time, including your brother's team. With your lady waiting at the train station, she can't interrupt this time."

"Nartan, do you think this is safe?"

"Ikshu, I will be next to you every step of the way. If it gets dangerous, I promise to pull your spirit back to this plane in this timeline. You will have both healing events as you should have had last time. That is why it didn't work."

"Son, the first event is the exact moment you lost your voice to the trauma. The event that follows is where we change your perspective to take away the abandonment, betrayal, or shame. We will know which one when we analyze your symptoms during the first event." My teacher looks to me with promise in his eyes. I sit down with my hands in my lap to hear them without my anger filling my ears.

"Symptoms? How would I know? I was a terrified kid?"

"Not your symptoms living it then, your symptoms living it a second time," Nartan says with an eye roll. Condescending Nartan is a familiar comfort. Supportive Nartan shook me to my core, and I'm glad he's buried inside my brother's hardened shell. We nod at one another.

"Okay, if you let Nartan lead, I consent."

"What's wrong with these descendants of ours? They pick the least experienced to lead them and then scream to high heavens when everything ends up tail over ears," quips one of Nartan's spirit team members.

165

"Son, lay down and relax your breathing. You will fall into a meditative state again," Teacher says. He has changed into full ceremonial garb and carries a feather smudge fan. Behind him, Nartan's spirit team members are also in their ritual costumes. They hold larger smudge fans of feathers and bags representing the bag the Creator carried when our earth was made.

My breathing slows. The men chant a guttural rhythm in our language but too fast to be interpreted. I guess I'm not meant to know the words only to feel the power of their magic. Nartan leads the spirits in a stomping pattern in my small space. Golden light glows on his path and floats to the low rise of the bed. If I didn't know better, I would think my brother moved the sun to rotate under us, or perhaps he moved us to its surface.

Inside me, my spirit jolts awake. I step out of my body to collide with Nartan's entourage. "Get in line, turkey. Younglings in the back, and you haven't the rings on you to compete with these geezers." The warning comes from one of his guides as they push me to the back. I stomp behind them with half their grace and one-tenth of Nartan's suave moves.

"That's it, son. Follow their lead." The praise of my teacher warms my heart. He is grinning at me over his shoulder as the last man in line. The teepee swirls and tilts as we astral travel to another teepee burnt long ago.

Grandmother Winter sits on her perch sewing while I struggle to thread a brush. I would be embarrassed to have Nartan see my tongue-loose concentration over my task, but he never saw value in my talents at that age. He defended me against those braves who sought to beat me, but he never approved of my handicrafts until Olive took an interest in selling them.

The hoofbeats from my nightmares start their staccato rhythm. My adult form moans as the familiar aching in my chest intensifies. I'm in my nightmare…as two selves…again. This time, I know to watch Grandmother Winter. She sits up before the hoofbeats should have reached her ancient ears. She looks to another place in the teepee. I follow her line of sight to where my teacher stands. I thought she was looking at me because we were side by side in the last healing.

Now he's across the room. She senses him and searches for his spiritual presence, not mine. When their gazes connect, he smiles and puts a fist over his heart. Does she smile back? The lines on her face prevent me from being sure, but I think she's smiling. She places a hand over the brush my child self was making. She whispers her warning.

The lighted stick thumps across the top of the teepee, which starts the fire. The spirit team stomps around the red, hot cinders raining on us. My child self jumps up and grabs Grandmother by the elbows. Her shoulders buckle, not because of the force of my impotent frame, but because she was staring at my teacher. Reality had faded for her. "Come, Grandmother, we must leave. Something about this fire scares me. Please let's go," my little voice cries.

"My beautiful wife, I have come to collect you. Tonight, you shall die to take your place at my side, but first, you must send our dear Ikshu on his way. You will see him again, but I must have you to myself first," whispers my teacher.

Of course, he is Grandfather Winter, and this is where he claims his soulmate for the next life. How did I miss the connection? Jealousy burns inside me hotter than the burning canvas surrounding us. She smiles at my teacher with a toothless grin. This one lights her whole face. How did I overlook her smile all these years? She mouths at him, and he puts his other hand over his heart.

"You mustn't speak. You must not let them find you. Promise me you will be silent as you crawl out of the back of the teepee. Promise!" she yells at my child self while shaking me by the shoulders.

"Ikshu, are your hands hot or cold?" Nartan's question is bewildering. We are stomping around a burning teepee. I brush my hand under my chin.

"My hand is ice cold." Shock slows my words and confuses my feet. I stumble and step out of the path of the other dancers. The last thing I need is to throw away my sanity because I led the spirit team into a pile-on.

"Son, it is time to turn this from a traumatic event to a healing event. Are you ready?"

I nod at him as tears fill my eyes. I have never had support and love swirling around me in this terrible place. My body begins to shake as the memory changes from Grandmother Winter abandoning me with the instruction to be silent. It is changing to the day the invaders returned her to her soulmate for safekeeping until their next life together.

Nartan's face fills my view, and his hands press down on my shoulders. The weight of the world rests in his grip. "Ikshu, you did the best you could with what you had at the time. There is no guilt in surviving. It was the outcome destined to befall Grandmother Winter just as you were meant to escape." His stern delivery leaves me no room to argue. The intensity in his eyes reassures the frightened child inside of me. "You know what to do," he says in his hypnotic voice.

"Run, Ikshu. It's too late for her. Run! Climb a tree and wait for Nartan!" My yell comes out as a series of sobs, but my child self-snaps out of his shock. He turns the opposite direction of the hand and struggles with the ties at the bottom of the teepee. Nartan lifts a ceremonial knife from his belt and hands it to me. I cut the ties to give my child self the hole he needs to escape. The boy dives through the opening and runs into the night.

"Follow him," Nartan says before unleashing a battle cry of fury. His team echoes the cry and rushes from the teepee crossing through the canvas like the ghosts they are—only my brother crosses too. The ease of his movement from spirit to corporeal to spirit again sends shivers down my spine. How can Olive know the power he yields over life and death, and yet, sass him continuously?

I dive through the hole we made in the teepee and catch up with my younger, weaker self. I use Nartan's magical knife to cut hanging branches, protruding tree roots, and poisonous vines in the path of the boy. He's running forward but facing back toward the fire. I hit his back with a discarded branch to keep him on the cleared path. At one point, he is stalked by a cougar, but I run to the beast while waving my arms. The cat doesn't know what to do with the phantom energy field and leaves the boys alone.

We get to the tree I remember was my hiding place, but the boy doesn't climb it. He stops at its base and wails in agony. "Oh no, oh no," I beg the boy. "You don't know it, but they are looking for you. They will catch you down here. Why aren't you climbing?" I will throw him into the tree if I must. This tree has edible berries in it, waxy leaves to shelter him from the coming rain, and thick foliage to hide him. It's perfect. I thought I knew that when I climbed it. In my panic, I reach for him.

Grandfather Winter grabs me by the shoulders. "Don't touch him! He will drop dead," he whispers tersely in my ear. My teacher climbs the tree and grabs a handful of berries. They turn black with rot at his touch, and the surrounding leaves wither and die on contact. He rains the dead berries onto our heads.

The boy looks up.

A whistle sounds in the distance. Then one man shouts to another. Our time from Nartan's diversion is running out. Luckily, the boy scrambles up the tree. I breathe a sigh of relief and bend at the waist to hug my knees.

"It is done," Grandfather Winter says with a pat on my back. "See, you did the best you could with what you had at the time. It wasn't your silence that saved you. It was your speed, your strength, and most of all your courageous spirit."

My eyes snap open and I'm back on my bed. Nartan stomps alone in my teepee, chanting in our native language. He beats a drum with the handle of the feathered smudge fan I swear my teacher was holding. The weight around my heart is gone and my throat is clear. Will it stay this way once I'm surrounded by the folks at the station? I sit up to ask him a thousand questions before I'm struck with the power of his stare.

"I want my knife back before you go storm the train station," he says, choking back tears. He opens his arms, and I hug him with all my might.

Chapter 20

"We know what's best for you." Finn's words echo in my ears. They bounce around my skull and join the sounds of the train station hammering my brain. The other passengers stare at us. I let them gawk, but I don't give them the satisfaction of seeing my tears. I want to rage at them for whispering about Little Unwanted Ava who was jilted by Ikshu Sagebrush.

Little Ava whose family couldn't get rid of her fast enough. Maybe I'll become a spinster just to spite everyone. They can be responsible for me for the rest of my life since I can't be trusted to handle it on my own.

Who am I kidding? I'll be a spinster because I will never find anyone else compatible with my prickly ways. I'm picky. I'm difficult. I'm plain-spoken. Even my pretty face and heiress status isn't enough to outweigh my defensive habits and manly interests.

I don't belong in high society, but it's where my family wants me to be. My gloved fingers reach for the arm wheel I received from Ikshu. I had to wear it today. I may never take it off. The beads roll over my skin in a loving caress, and if I close my eyes, I see his fingers gliding over me.

I had thought Ikshu accepted me, but now I see I wasn't enough. He will be haunted by the deeds of those with my skin color forever. If only I could make him whole. He spoke freely to me in private, and I thought we were a team. Then he fainted when I needed him most. Even Nartan agreed with my brothers, it would be best for all involved if we were separated. I push the conversation as we left the Sagebrush Homestead to the dark corners of my mind to keep from crying.

Goodbye, Ikshu.

I sniffle and take my handkerchief from my journal where it was holding my place. I dab my eyes and nose like a lady when I wish to throw the material over my head to hide. Sketches of his face and descriptions of his mannerisms stare back at me from the journal pages. Someday I will have to burn this book.

Choo! The train's whistle blasts over our heads. I lift my chin like an ancient priestess headed to a sacrifice. My father reaches for a hug and I stand stiffly. I march past my brothers' open arms without a look. Once this train leaves, I am never coming back. Jealousy boils in my belly at the women who live here happily with their chosen men. Anyone receiving a kiss goodbye gets a glare from me. I don't deserve this life. Everyone says so.

Up the three steps, through the doors, and along six rows, I go to a window seat facing the station platform. One last indulgence, I open my journal and run my finger over Ikshu's smile. This picture is his secret smile, the one lighting his face while he's working. I have never seen a man so happy at work. Listening to my brothers grumbling, I didn't think loving your responsibilities was possible.

"Is this seat taken?" A rotund woman holding a large plant smacks my shoulder. I don't know which makes her a worse traveling companion, the nasal soprano of her voice or her plant's spiky fronds big enough to span the aisle. When I don't respond, she repeats herself while leaning over my shoulder. The tinny sound grates against my eardrums, and I cover my ears with my hands before I can censor myself.

"I guess not," she says and plops into the aisle seat. I'm crushed against the window with the prospect of dueling with a plant as my only means of entertainment. The giant white feathers of her hat bob with her movement and smack my head repeatedly as she settles. I am slapped in the shoulder with a small leather pouch at her side.

Beads adorn it in a pattern that matches the giant plant in her arms. I choke back a sob. This is one of the pouches Ikshu made and sold at the tobacco shop. I sniffle in self-pity. The plant smells herbal. *Oh no.* It is sagebrush. My eyes cloud with tears, and I beg the train to leave. I am holding myself together with hairpins and false bravado.

"AVA! AVA!" My name is yelled outside. I smoosh my face against the window glass. I know that voice, but it cannot be. He never speaks above a whisper. Did I get knocked out by plant or hat protrusion? I must be dreaming.

He's calling for me.

Ikshu rides FoolsGold up and down the train platform, screaming my name. Railway employees and my brothers chase him along the platform. He deftly out-maneuvers them while dodging frightened travelers. Women scream. Men yell they are being robbed. Chaos reigns. I laugh with glee.

Ikshu Sagebrush came to my rescue, and no one can escape the spectacle. They can gossip all they want about my love story as long as I end up riding into the sunset with him.

"AVA!"

"Of all the delays," my traveling companion snorts behind her monstrous plant.

"Can I get through? I need to get out," I say, standing over her. Barbs from the plant score the bodice of my dress. The red tatters hang from its tips as if it draws first blood.

"We are about to leave," she quips. She shifts the plant onto the knee closest to me and cuts my space in half. She pulls out a map and pretends to study it.

Panic closes my chest and threatens to squeeze my heart to bursting. I will not miss him. I look for an escape. The train is full. If I climb over the seats, I will hurt someone. I'm trapped. I'm suffocating.

"AVA!"

"She's gone, you scoundrel," Fletcher yells. "Be a gentleman and let her go!"

My stomach rolls with panic. I cannot freeze with an attack and miss my chance at happiness. I fight through the mental fog. *No, no, no.* My chest constricts with an impending panic attack from the enclosed, noisy space. I must get fresh air before I pass out. I bang my fist on the window to get someone's attention on the platform. Ikshu? Dad? The frantic chase with shrieking obstacles steals everyone's focus from the train. *Choo!* The whistle to pull away blows again.

The deafening sound of the train's pistons turning the wheels is a death march.

I pat around the edges of the window to discover it latches at the top. I struggle to gain purchase on the rusted edges and slide open the locks. My nails puncture the fingertips from my gloves. The gloves unravel as I wrestle the window half-open. I lean my torso out as far as I dare.

"Ikshu, I'm over here!" I scream like a banshee and wave my shredded glove as a white flag of surrender. He zeros in on my voice over the deafening noise of the platform. Our eyes meet. I reach for him and wobble on my perch.

****

Over the chaos, her voice calls to me like a mythical siren to the sailors in her books. These people need to move. I do not want to run them over, but they stand in the open. I fight to turn FoolsGold whose temperament is not compatible with the scene on the platform. As the passengers raise their voices, he becomes distracted. I smooth his mane with my palm to remind him of our connection.

"Ava, I came for you," I yell. I love the clarity and power of my voice. The expression of pride on her face reaches to my soul and warms its icy exterior. Then she falters and tips toward the ground. If she falls from that height onto the tracks, she will break her bones.

She twists to grab onto the window frame which shoves her backside through the square hole. She clings to the top of the window, feet dangling inside the train, but her seat dangling outside of it. I ride to her side, but even on horseback, I am too short to reach her. "Choose me, Ava. Let go of the train and drop into my arms. I will never let you fall," I swear with all my heart.

She nods, and the train lurches forward. It starts to move. She clings to the window in fear. I walk FoolsGold at the pace of the train. "Marry me, Ava. Will you let go of the train to be my wife?"

"I want to be yours. Ikshu, I'm afraid—I looked

down. The train is moving. I can't jump." Her voice shakes as hard as her body. Her face is ashen with tears painting streaks down each cheek. She clings to the train with terror.

I place my knee to FoolsGold's back and boost myself to kneeling. I grab her around the waist and haul her from the train. She lets go long enough to latch onto my shoulders. She buries her face in my chest with a whimper. My horse stops at the end of the platform. I kiss her forehead and thank the Creator for the chance to hold my Ava once more. She burrows deeper to seek comfort in my embrace. Masculine pride fills my spirit, and I vow to always be her haven.

"I am sorry I was late, Ava. I had to find myself first."

"Ikshu Sagebrush, what in tarnation do you think you are doing?" Sheriff Hansen's voice brings me crashing back to earth. The aging Sheriff more waddles than limps. Despite his diseased state, he holds the power between life and hanging. It is time to speak up and claim my future wife.

"Just picking up my intended at the train station, sir. There seems to be some confusion on whether or not she is traveling today." Ava giggles and snorts into my tunic which, hopefully, I'm the only one to hear.

"The only confusion, young man, was caused by you. Someone could have been hurt. Look around you. This platform is in chaos because of your antics," Finn's face blazes red with anger. He clenches his fists at his sides. If I dismount, one of those fists will likely connect with my face.

"Grand statements come with grand gestures. I couldn't let her leave before she decided whether or not

176

to accept my proposal."

"Proposal?" The Wylder family exchanges wide-eyed looks with raised eyebrows.

"Is it so hard to believe I have fallen for her? She's beautiful, smart, witty, and accepting of my family." I release the tension on my arms to lean her away from my chest. I stare into her storm-cloud eyes. "Ava, I don't have a manor, a title, or a lavish lifestyle to offer you, but I will love you more than the champions in your books. You will be a working wife, but I will be working at your side. I will listen more than I talk because that's my nature. I offer you a lifetime of silence to enjoy nature's beauty together."

She raises her head, leaving tear tracks on my tunic. She looks to her family and says, "He loves me. I won't leave our love behind."

"Ava, you would be throwing away all you have worked toward. Are you sure?" Her father's words threaten to momentarily stop my heart. Will he back her choice?

"Dad, I threw myself out of a train window for him," she says with a sniffle.

"I only ever wanted you to be happy. I promised your mother I would keep all you kids happy."

"Sir, I promise on every family member who came before me, everything that I am, and everything I shall be, your daughter's happiness is my soul's mission. My sun will rise and set with her whims. She will want for nothing, and I will move heaven and earth to see her smile."

"That's a bit much," scowls Finn.

"He's as melodramatic as she is," Fletcher mutters. "They deserve each other."

"Ava, is this the life you choose?" Her father's voice drips with expectation.

I set her onto FoolsGold's saddle to climb down. I wish to face her father on equal footing. Proud as a princess, Ava addresses him down her nose. "Daddy, what did Mom say when she climbed to your window to convince you to elope? I want to say those words to you now. Your blessing means the world to me, but I am cut from the same cloth as Mom. We will be married today if I have to drag every one of you to the church or run west like you did, Father."

"Love me," her father says with tears in his eyes. He folds his hat in his hands and shuffles his shoes. "All your mother asked was for me to love her the night we eloped. I followed her to watch what she would do next because every day was an adventure."

"Then love me enough to give me my choice of adventure."

He nods while her brothers gape in shock.

When I reach to help her from my horse, she shocks me by swinging her legs over my arms. She chooses to slide into my embrace over standing on her two feet. I'm left standing before her family with her body nestled against mine. "Finding our normal will be the adventure of a lifetime," she says before cupping my jaw in her palm. She guides my face toward hers and pours her fire into a scorching kiss. My face flames when the people on the platform applaud.

Epilogue

Who knew babies made so much noise? With luck, it is because these miniature monsters are black bear shifters like their mother and my babies will be quieter. Little Winter Sagebrush looks content in Ava's arms, but he hasn't stopped making baby gurgles since his birth. The cherub grabbed Ava's finger when she was tucking his blanket around him, and he hasn't let go. He takes after his uncle in that regard. Once I had Ava's heart, I vowed to never let go.

"Why, Mrs. Ava Sagebrush, you look a dream with a Sagebrush baby in your arms," I whisper against her shoulder. Tendrils of golden hair wave with my breath. She shivers beneath the caress. With any luck, it will be our baby celebrated in our cabin this time next year. However, we will not be having triplets. I don't envy my brother in the slightest. Hear that Great Creator and spirit team? No triplets for Ikshu and Ava. Thank you very much.

Even Little Sparrow Sagebrush, who is much smaller than his brother, is making his presence known. He stares from my embrace with Nartan's powerful gaze and condescending expression. I didn't think babies developed expressions until they were older. How can he already be a mini-Nartan? With that attitude, he is going to be a troublemaker. I can't wait to see the mischief he makes with his brothers and how my brother tries to control them.

Nartan has been running between his two rooms for over twenty-four hours. His spirit guides alternate between dancing with healing chants and making fun of him. It was frightening after Winter was born and Sparrow was struggling, knowing Moon was trapped inside during the drama. My stoic brother cried for hours before Sparrow's shoulders were finally free. Nartan's spirit team assured both of us, Sparrow was not injured in the birth. Now they stomp in an intricate pattern to the beat of Olive's screams. I cuddle Sparrow with gratitude that he seems to be alright. His tiny fist flies from his blanket bundle with unerring accuracy.

"Ouch, be gentle with your uncle," I whisper with a grunt of discomfort. I absently rub my rib which sets my new tattoo on fire. "Your father took a little too much pleasure in tattooing my rings last week. They are still sore."

Ava rolls her eyes at me, but she didn't see Nartan's expression as he stabbed me repeatedly with the cactus needles. I will grow to love the two rings I wear, but I fear never as much as my brother loved putting them there.

Next door, the bedroom goes quiet.

Nartan's team hums with heads bowed together. Ava stuffs her fist in her mouth to keep from crying out. Grandfather and Grandmother Winter appear at the bedroom doorway. His arm is looped over her shoulders as he stands tall and proud. Their lines of experience have melted away, so they look to be my age. Grandmother blows a kiss into the bedroom.

A baby cries.

The spirits step aside as Nartan rushes in with a pink

squealing infant held over his head. "Meet Moon Sagebrush," he calls. His deep voice shakes the walls of the cabin.

"Nartan Sagebrush, get back here this instant!" Olive's cry of fury startles my brother, and he runs back to the bedroom. Ava and I giggle at Olive's ability to humble the great spiritual leader to a pile of mush.

"While we are alone, I wanted to apologize for last night. I don't know what happened to trigger my nightmare, but I'm glad you were there on the other side of our divider. You chased the demons away so I could fall back asleep. Spiritual healing is a process which can take months or even years. I don't deserve someone as understanding, caring, and patient as you, darling."

"My sweet Ikshu, you don't have to thank me for being by your side. It was your first nightmare in over two months. I understand setbacks are going to happen as you work with Nartan to release your fears. If you trust in me to support you, we will navigate this together. Our relationship is not so fragile as to be ruined by broken sleep. You call, and my heart answers, asleep or not."

I wrap my free arm around her shoulders and squeeze her to my side. Sparrow reaches out and grips Winter's hair. The boys begin to wail while we untangle tiny fingers tipped with ferocious claws.

"I love you, Mrs. Sagebrush." She blushes and grants me her secret smile. This smile only comes out when I call her by my last name. This expression tells me how she loves to be my wife. I will earn her love every day as long as I live.

"Oh, Ikshu I—" Ava's affirmation is cut off by a loud rumble from the baby in her arms. A putrid cloud rises from Winter. The blanket bundle in Ava's arms develops a yellow stain. Ava's soft expression curls into a devious smile as Nartan returns. I have learned to step back when my wife makes that face.

"Moon Sagebrush came into this world with a voracious appetite. Despite being the last to appear, he is the first to eat. Not surprising since he is the largest Sagebrush baby by far," Nartan announces with pride glowing from his eyes.

"Good timing because Winter needs your attention. He has signaled he needs his father," Ava says in a syrupy sweet voice. My gullible brother rushes to her side and swipes the baby from her arms. Ava quickly grabs Sparrow and retreats behind my back.

"Winter, what is it? How can I aid you, my son?" Winter makes a gurgling noise and releases more toxic fumes. Nartan's nose crinkles, and his proud smile melts into an ominous frown. Ava's laughter is music to my ears. I can't hold back and join her, much to Nartan's annoyance. He disappears into the bedroom.

"Nartan, how dare you ask me to change one while feeding the other! I don't care who you are or what your station is. Today, you are tailclout changer number one! Don't make that face at me!" Olive's yells only fuel our laughter. Several of Nartan's spirit guides are doubled over while one rolls on the floor with laughter at Nartan's fate.

"Thank you, Ikshu," Ava says before nuzzling Sparrow.

"For what?"

"For rescuing me and for making me a part of this family. This is the second happiest day of my life." Tears of joy shine in her storm-cloud eyes.

"Second? When was the first?"

"The first will be the day I hold your baby in my arms, love."

"I thought it was the day you threw yourself out of a train window and dragged every man in your life to the preacher, grumbling and complaining."

"I don't remember you complaining."

"I was. It must have been too quiet for you to hear it." I try to school my face, but a smile fights its way through.

"Oh really," she says with a raised eyebrow. With a baby in the crook of one arm and the other arm on her hip, she looks like my wildest dream come true. "What were the complaints I missed?"

"We couldn't cross town fast enough with those impractical settler shoes on your feet. How many pairs of boots must I make for you to wear them?" I can hardly get the words out between gaffs and laughs.

"I wasn't going to run. You already had me."

"It doesn't matter because I would have traveled across time and space to find you again. Fate crossed our paths at the Christmas party because we were destined to be husband and wife."

"How can you be so sure?" The teasing notes in her voice fade to reverence.

I look to Grandmother and Grandfather Winter who are embracing in the corner while watching the scene unfold. "That's what soulmates do, Ava. Our love astral traveled to this lifetime, following one small thread of energy to find one another. It will do so over and over because we are meant to be."

Ava's tentative kiss ignites the fire in my belly I associate with her. Tiny sips and pecks turn into dueling of tongues. I can't resist tangling my fingers in her hair and tilting her to deepen the kiss. We worship one another until Nartan's throat-clearing interrupts us.

"Moon is asleep. Winter is feeding, so I can take Sparrow now. I need you to mend the hole in the barn roof from the weight of the snow. I knew that corner was weakening, but I thought it would last until we start your cabin this spring."

"Should I go now or wait for you to climb up with me?"

"Me? Ikshu, I have three newborns, and I haven't slept in days. I'm taking a nap. Besides, you have all you need to fix it…a partner who is an expert at climbing the side of our barn." Nartan flashes a knowing smile, and Ava turns as red as a tomato.

As usual, my brother is right. As long as I have Ava at my side, I have everything I need.

A word about the author…

Marilyn Barr currently resides in the wilds of Kentucky with her husband, son, and rescue cats. When engaging with the real world, she is collecting characters, empty coffee cups, and unused homeschool curricula. She has a diverse background containing experiences as a child prodigy turned medical school reject, biodefense microbiologist, high school science teacher, homeschool mother of a savant and advocate for the autistic community. Only her passion for books rivals her passion for pizza. She would love to hear from readers via her website www.marilynbarr.com.

http://www.marilynbarr.com

Lightning Source UK Ltd.
Milton Keynes UK
UKHW021937031022
409880UK00020B/245